IRON LEGACY

An Outlaw Biker Tale

Alex McRae

Published by Iron Battalion Press

Made in the USA

2025

Visit Alex McRae at www.alexmcrae.net to sign up to the author's newsletter and learn more about Iron Battalion books.

Twitter : @AlexMcRae99

Instagram: @alexmcrae99

Amazon : https://www.amazon.com/stores/Alex-McRae/author/B0F344WTHB

CHAPTER 1

Rex had gotten the call, and he was summoned to Banner Hospital in Tucson by his motorcycle club president. As he weaved his way through the afternoon's traffic on his Harley, he was followed by his best friend in the whole world, Clay "Hawk" Hawkins. He had known Clay since junior high; they had always shared their love of motorcycles and had even joined their club, The Steel Reapers, at the same time.

Clay was a skilled rider but not the sharpest knife in the drawer, yet he followed Rex with ease. Countless hours on the road riding in formation at very high speeds will give you that discipline. No fancy riding school could teach you that stuff. It was not given to you, and you had to earn it. With their club, the Steel Reapers, they had crisscrossed the country hundreds of times, getting into all sorts of hijinks on the way. It was a good life, and Rex loved it. Forever Two Wheels.

Rex had somewhat of a clue as to why he was told to be at this hospital this afternoon. One of the old-timers in the club, Eli "Iron Hand" McCallum, was dying and had requested that Rex and Clay meet with him. Eli was a world-class custom motorcycle builder and one of the Old Guard in the Steel Reapers. His scoots were admired worldwide. He had won countless awards for his builds, and pretty much everything he built in the last five years was bought by some high-end collector in Japan. Who knew that they had such an appreciation of old pan heads and shovel heads over there?

Rex didn't know why Eli had sent for him and Clay, but he had a feeling he would soon find out. In the back of his mind, he hoped that Eli was gifting him some rare chopper, but that was just wishful thinking. He had been close with Eli but not THAT close. So, it had to be something else. Why Clay, as well? Was Clay tight with Eli? He tried to think back on occasions the two had hung out together, but nothing really sprang to mind.

He saw the signs ahead for Banner Medical Center and started slowing down as he didn't want to miss the turn-off. Just like that, Clay followed his lead and blipped down through his gears as well. The two rode in sync, like some unspoken language between them. They cruised through the car park until they found a spot near enough to the front doors of the hospital and managed to squeeze both their bikes into the same spot. Rex shut off his Harley and pulled off his helmet. He waited for Clay to do the same and turned and asked him.

"Any idea why Eli wants to see us, bro?"

"I dunno. I heard he ain't got long to go now. Maybe he wants to give us two of those world-famous choppers of his." Clay replied, "I really loved that purple-flaked pan head that won all those awards at the Iron Horizons Chopper Fest in Scottsdale last year."

Rex cast his mind back to that chopper. Yeah, she was a beaut. A real work of art. From memory, that had sold for over $125,000 in the end. Crazy money but well worth it.

"He sold that one, dumbass," Rex scolded his buddy.

"Yeah, I know," sighed Clay. "But just saying, if I could have my pick and choose any of his creations, that would be the one."

"Hmmpf, fair enough," Rex replied. "Let's go in and find Eli then, eh?"

"Yeah, let's do this thing," Clay replied, leaving his helmet on his handlebars and walking towards the front entrance of the hospital.

They hit the front desk of the hospital and asked the duty nurse where they could find Eli McCallum. She told them the ward number and explained how to get there.

Of course, as soon as they hit the bank of elevators, they both totally forgot everything she had said, and they spent the next 20 minutes getting lost all over the hospital. Not a good start. Finally, they found the ward. The cancer ward. Oh shit. This doesn't look good, Rex thought to himself.

Rex and Clay studied the sign as they stepped into the ward to figure out where they could find Eli. A worried ward nurse spotted them and hurried over.

"Can I help you, gentlemen?" she asked fairly frostily.

"Yeah, we are looking for Eli McCallum," Rex explained.

The nurse looked at the clock on the wall and huffed. "Only family are allowed in at this time. Are you family?" she asked.

Without missing a beat, Rex replied, "Yeah, we are his sons."

Clay was about to say something. Rex slid his biker boot into Clay's foot.

"Ow," yelped Clay.

The nurse studied them some more. "You don't look like brothers," she finally said.

Again, without missing a beat, Rex lied, "Yeah, same dad, different moms."

"Well, that would explain it. Follow me, please." She walked down past the main desk for this floor of the hospital and took a quick right down another sterilized white hallway. The floor was so spotless you could have eaten your dinner off it, Rex noted.

"Room 4B, on your left," the nurse pointed down the hall. "Don't get him upset, and you have 30 minutes. I'll come by then to check on him." The way she looked at them both made Rex feel like she was saying she would check on them more.

"Yeah, okay, thanks," Rex replied dismissively. The pair continued down the hall as the nurse eyed them suspiciously.

"Geez, what's up with her?" asked Clay. "It's like she thinks we are going to kill him or something. Doesn't she know we are club brothers?"

"I guess not," Rex shrugged. "C'mon, let's go see Eli."

They quickly found the door to room 4B and hustled their way in. As soon as they entered, Rex was in shock; Eli was hooked up to a bank of machines all bleeping and whirring away to themselves. He had on an oxygen mask, and he was a husk of a man. Coming into the Steel Reapers in their early 20s, Eli was already in his mid-40s, 6 ft 1, and 210 lbs of solid muscle; now, he looked like a frail old man strapped into all of these medical devices keeping him alive.

Eli looked up at the pair, and it was almost like it took his brain a moment to figure out who they were.

"Eli, it's us," Rex blurted out. "Rex and Hawk, your club brothers. You remember us."

Eli squinted and wheezed, then adjusted himself in his hospital bed. He pulled off his oxygen mask and gestured for them to come closer.

"Of course, I remember you, Wolf, you too, Clay," he wheezed. "Thanks for coming to see me."

"Of course, brother, you call, and we come. You know that," Clay replied.

Rex looked at him. Who gave you permission to speak?

"How are you holding up?" asked Rex, eyeing the myriad of machines Eli was strapped into.

'Not good, boys. I reckon I got a day or two, and I am done," Eli replied.

"Fuck, man, sorry to hear it," said Rex. "Cancer, right?"

"Yeah, from smoking," Eli wheezed. "I survived being shot, stabbed, bashed, and wouldn't you know it. Cancer got me."

"Sorry, man, sorry," was all Rex could think of to say. It felt like anything he could say at this point was just lip service. Nothing could make it better for old Eli.

'It started in my lungs and spread to my spine and my brain," Eli continued. "Too late to operate, boys."

'Sorry, man," Rex replied. "If there is anything we can do for you, just name it."

Eli groaned again, clearly in a lot of pain. "Yes, there is, actually. Pass me my wallet, would ya?" He pointed to a dresser drawer just out of reach of his hospital bed.

Rex pulled the drawer open to spy on some of Eli's belongings. Some photographs, a lighter, sunglasses, his favorite riding gloves, and a well-worn and battered leather wallet.

"Here ya go, brother." Rex offered the wallet to the bedridden old man.

"Thanks," Eli wheezed again. He fished through the wallet until he found a solitary key and a scrap of paper. He then proceeded to hand the wallet back to Rex so he could return it to the drawer.

Once Rex returned his wallet, he turned to see Eli holding up the solitary key.

"Come closer," Eli asked. Rex moved in closer to the hospital bed to hear what Eli had to say.

"This key," Eli struggled with his breathing to get the sentence out. "Is the key to a lock-up behind my bike shop? Do not lose it." He handed the key to Rex.

"Okay, I got you, brother," Rex replied, pocketing the key into the back of his jeans.

"In that lock-up is a custom bike. I want you to give it to my daughter."

Rex was shocked. He never knew Eli had any kids, let alone a daughter. In all the years of knowing Eli, he had never heard him speak about family members. He played his cards close to his chest, but he didn't have a clue that Eli had kids.

"Sure, sure, of course," Rex stammered. "We can do that for you."

"You can count on us," Clay added. "We won't let you down."

"Promise me she will get that bike. Please," begged Eli.

'Of course, of course," Rex replied. "How do we find her?"

"Here, this is her last known address." Eli handed a scrap of well-worn paper to Rex. Rex unfolded it and studied it. Clay peered in over Rex's shoulder to get a closer look.

"Pine Hollow, Arizona? Where's that?" asked Clay. "Never heard of it."

Eli groaned and moved about in his bed. Rex shot Clay a dirty look.

'White Mountains," he wheezed. "She lives in the White Mountains near Show Low."

"Ok, got it," Rex replied, trying to sound confident. "Retrieve the bike from your lock-up. Take it to the White Mountains. Find your daughter and give it to her. Don't worry, brother, we won't let you down."

"You promise?" asked Eli, clearly in pain.

"We promise, man. We will do this for you," Rex reassured.

'Thank you. Thank you," Eli replied, rolling in his bed.

The snooty nurse who had told them where Eli's room was earlier popped her head into the room.

"5 minutes, boys. You've got 5 more minutes, then you will have to leave."

Rex looked back at her. "Okay. Okay, no problem, lady."

"We should probably leave," Clay suggested.

Rex leaned over Eli in his bed. "Listen to me, brother. We have the key; we have her address. We will do this for you. Do not worry. We won't let you down."

"Thank you," Eli replied before closing his eyes and grimacing in pain. "I know you won't let me down."

CHAPTER 2

Rex and Clay said their goodbyes to the ailing Eli and exited the hospital. The duty nurse kept a close eye on them until they left the ward and returned to the main elevators. They exited the building and walked through the car park back to their bikes.

'Phew, that was intense," Clay announced.

'Yeah, brutal. Poor bastard, he's in really bad shape," Rex replied. "I never even knew he had a daughter, did you?"

"Nup, no way," Clay replied. 'Thought he was a carefree bachelor."

'Yeah. Who knew?" asked Rex.

"Right," Rex replied. "So let's get some food; I'm starving."

"Me too," Clay replied. "I saw a Denny's on the ride in. Let's hit that."

"Sounds good," Rex replied, grabbing his helmet from his handlebars.

Rex followed Clay through the surface roads of Tucson to this Denny's, which he claimed he had spotted on the way in. Clay weaved his way in and out of traffic for a couple of blocks before signaling Rex to pull to the right. They parked their bikes, entered the diner, and took a booth near the back to keep an eye on everyone coming and going from this fine dining establishment.

'So what do you think?" Clay asked Rex.

"About what? Eli dying? Incredibly sad. I thought that guy was invincible."

"Well, he was back in the day," Clay replied. "I meant about this bike for her daughter."

"Oh, that. Yeah, of course. We can take the van up. Have a night in Phoenix, head north, drop it off, and be home in what? 3-4 days," Rex replied. "Easy peasy."

"Sounds good. How far are the White Mountains from Phoenix?" Clay asked.

"About 4 hours from memory," Rex replied. "I can get some time off work next week; what about you?"

"Bro, I'm on unemployment right now; I can go next week, no problem," Clay replied.

Rex had forgotten that Clay had recently been laid off from his job. 'Or maybe we can aim for the week after that?"

"Yeah, just let me know!" Clay replied.

CHAPTER 3

As they ate their burgers, Rex and Clay talked about growing up with Eli.

20 years back, when they were both 17, they started drinking at one of Tucson's most notorious Biker bars, The Rogues Refuge. Despite being underage, as long as you showed up there on a motorcycle, the barmaids would serve you.

Rex and Clay both owned Honda Shadow 600s and were the kings of their local High School. Every Friday and Saturday night, they would hit the Rogues and soak up the atmosphere. This was the bar the notorious Steel Reapers drank at. The Reapers gave them no hassle and would often nod at them as they sat in their little booth near the front doors of the bar.

One Saturday night, they entered the bar and bought two Bud Lights from their favorite barmaid. They took their usual position, their little booth by the doors. The only Steel Reaper they could see drinking in there was Eli. Rex was sure the rest of the club would show up a little later as they always held court at the Rogues on a Saturday night.

Loud rock music blared through the dive bar, and a few biker old ladies were dancing away by the small stage. The front doors swung open, and to Rex and Clay's surprise, 5 members of the Hellbound Nomads (a small Tucson-based Outlaw Motorcycle Club) came swaggering in. Almost immediately, you could feel the tension in the air. Rex kicked Clay's biker boot under the table. The gesture was clear: "Be ready."

The 5 made their way to the bar and soon ordered whiskey shots and beer chasers. They turned their respective backs to the bar and eyed the patrons of the Rogues Refuge. Almost immediately, Eli put down his drink and walked up to them. Rex couldn't hear what was being said but assumed it was words to the effect, "This is a Steel Reaper bar, and you gotta leave."

He could tell by the body language that the Nomads had no intention of leaving. They had come in here to test the Reapers and show their dominance. To walk out now would show a loss of face and demonstrate their weakness. Besides, it was 5 on 1. Even the best fighters can't usually take out 5 guys. That was the Nomad's first mistake.

The biggest of the Nomads pushed Eli hard in the chest. He stepped back a foot, regained his balance, and, with a fast left jab, connected with the big guy's chin, sending the aggressor crumpling to the floor. 1 down, 4 to go. The remaining 4 Nomads rat-packed Eli, pummeling him with blows, most of them fairly ineffectual. Eventually, one of the Nomads got a grip on Eli's leather riding vest and flung him onto a table and bar stools. Eli was out. Clay looked at Rex like, "Shouldn't we do something?" Despite still being high school kids and more than likely they would get their asses handed to them if they stepped in, they hated to see a man heavily outnumbered like this. Rex held his hand up to Clay in a "hold on a sec" type gesture.

The Nomads helped their big friend to his feet as he regained consciousness. Rex could see from their position by the front doors that the Nomad guy was still wobbly. One of his club brothers handed him his beer, and he carefully took a sip. One of the smaller guys slapped the biker who had tossed Eli across the room on the back, laughing as he did so. *Big joke, five on one,* thought Rex.

The Nomads turned their back on the patrons and started talking to the barmaids, ordering more whiskey shots from what Rex could tell. Then, like something out of the horror movies when you thought the killer was finally dead, only for him to spring up to kill some more horny teenagers, Eli tossed the turned-over table to the side, grabbed a bar stool, and sprang up, to attack the Nomads again. The look of shock on their faces as he clobbered them repeatedly with one of the bar stools was priceless. Despite this being real violence and not movie violence happening right in front of Rex and Clay's eyes, there was almost something funny about it. Eli beat them back unmercifully.

One of the Nomads who Eli had beaten with a bar stool had gone down and was now getting up off the dive bar floor. He found himself at Eli's side and swung a wild right, catching Eli on the chin. The lone Reaper went down to the floor for the second time tonight. Instead of stopping the fight, the Nomads proceeded to kick him and spit on Eli, who downed Steel Reaper.

That was it for Rex, and you don't kick a man when he is down. He gestured to Clay, then he got up out of the booth and made straight for the Nomads. At this point in Rex's life, he had never been in a bar fight, only silly high school fights after school, which were usually broken up by a teacher leaving for the day. Unsure of what to do, he decided to just do a running kick into the back of the nearest Nomad, channeling his inner Chuck Norris. Undignified, but it worked; the man went down, knocking the wind out of his lungs. As one of the other Nomads turned to see who had attacked them, Clay came to the rescue, cracking a bar stool over the man's head and knocking him out.

Clay proceeded to continue swinging the bar stool wildly at the 3 remaining Nomads until one of the meaner-looking bikers grabbed the stool, wrenched it out of Clay's hands, and started peppering him with blows. Clay stepped back and back again as the angry Nomad rained down blows on Rex's 17-year-old buddy. Rex wasn't doing much better than Clay, with another of the Nomads grabbing his hair with his left hand and pounding Rex with his right fist. Rex attempted to block the grown man's fists with his left forearm and attempted to punch his assailant with his own right fist. It was only a matter of time till one of the Nomad's punches knocked Rex out. After all, he was just a skinny 17-year-old fighting off a grown-ass man.

To Rex's surprise, Eli sprang up again. He looked over and assessed the situation; two skinny teenagers had joined his fight. He nodded at Rex, grabbed the Nomad beating on the teen, and knocked him out with one punch. He pushed the Nomad behind that one out of the way and then grabbed the biker who was flailing on Clay in a headlock, choking the fight out of the man. Clay started punching the man in the face as Eli choked him.

At that very moment, 2 more Steel Reapers entered the Rogues Refuge. Their smiles left their faces the moment they realized what was going on, and the duo raced to help Eli get out of the melee. Soon, the Nomads were out-manned and outgunned. One of their men made a run for the door; on seeing the coward flee, two others staggered and followed him out the door. The two newcomer Steel Reapers grabbed the downed Nomads and unceremoniously tossed them out the door of the dive bar. Stunned and bloodied, Rex and Clay could think of nothing better than to start picking up chairs and tables and setting them upright. To this day, Rex isn't sure why they did that.

After consoling with Eli, one of the two new arrivals came over to Rex and Clay.

'Hey, you guys, what's your name?" the Outlaw biker asked.

Panting and out of breath, Rex introduced himself and Clay. The biker introduced himself as Hank. He invited the teens to sit at their table at the back of the bar. For helping Eli out in the fight, they were rewarded with free beers for the rest of the night. For the rest of the school year, all he and Clay would talk about was the night they helped the Steel Reapers beat the Hellbound Nomads down.

From that night on, the boys were always greeted with a warm welcome whenever they drank at the Refuge. They started getting invited to Steel Reaper parties and basically became hang-around. They soon learned that not only was Eli a top-level street fighter, but he also ran one of the best motorcycle custom shops in Tucson. They were invited around to his shop, and with his guidance, he had them customize their scoots. Even just simple changes to their Hondas VLX dramatically altered their bike's appearance. Ape hanger handlebars and peanut gas tanks were the first mods they learned. Eli showed them how to chop the back of their Softail frames and make their scoots hardtails. Once those mods had been made, it set them up for tall sissy bars. Impossible to install on softail scoots. Soon, they had the best-looking Honda's in Tucson.

After high school, they both had full-time jobs, so naturally, they upgraded to Harley's. Rex's first was a used Dyna, and Clay's a Sportster. In time, both young men were invited to prospect for the Steel reapers, finally earning their patches after a year's grueling hard work.

"That was pretty much our introduction to Eli," Clay reminisced.

'Yeah, I had never seen a guy walk up to 5 dudes and confront them before," Rex replied 'Most men would have sat and waited for backup."

"Yeah, that impressed the shit out of me back then," Clay added 'I had never seen anything like it."

"And now look at him," said Rex solemnly.

'Fuck Cancer," Clay retorted.

'Indeed," Rex replied.

They finished their burgers and cradled their sodas as they reflected on their years with the club. The waitress came and handed them their check, and Rex went to the counter to pay as Clay sat at their booth.

Rex returned and sat down. "I should probably get going soon," he said to Clay.

Before Clay had a chance to reply, Rex's cell phone went off. He looked down; it was their Steel Reaper Club president, Big John. He stuck his phone in front of Clay's face 'I should probably take this."

Clay nodded with a look of "Yeah, of course" on his face.

Rex took the call. Clay watched as Rex nodded and spoke the occasional 'Uh huh," and "Oh no," Eventually, he just said, "Shit, I'm sorry, John. Shit"

Clay could tell it was bad news. Rex hung up.

"Bad news, I assume?" Clay asked

'Yeah, man," Rex looked down at the table top. 'Eli just passed."

"What? Passed where?" Clay said confused

"Dude, he just died," Rex explained.

'But we just saw him an hour ago," Clay exclaimed.

'I know, I know. I was there," Rex replied. "You realize what this means, right?'

'What?" Clay asked.

'His request for us to take that bike to his daughter," Rex paused for effect. "It's a dying man's wish. We have to do it now."

'Shit, yeah, you are right," said Clay 'We gotta do this for sure."

"That settles it. I will talk to my boss on Monday and arrange for some time off, and then we will head to the White Mountains, track down his missing daughter, and fulfill our sworn duty."

'I agree," added Clay. "Just let me know when we are doing this, and I'll be ready."

The high school friends said their goodbyes and headed to their respective homes, promising to speak in a couple of days and put the plan into action.

CHAPTER 4

A week later, they met up at Rex's place, which had Clay's van and trailer attached to it. Clay already had his scoot tied up on the trailer.

"Hey, what's up with you bringing your bike?" Rex asked Clay, peering into the driver's side window of Clay's van.

'Yeah, so I looked it up online. The White Mountains have some great riding trails. I figure if we are taking Eli's daughter her bike, we might as well take advantage of the fact we are up there for a few days and get some riding in."

Rex contemplated Clay's logic. They already had one of the best scenic rides in the USA, the Tucson to Mount Lemmon run, but what the hell? Exploring new roads was half the reason to ride a Harley.

"Well, if you're bringing your scoot, I'll take mine too," Rex declared. "Let me grab my gear."

15 minutes later, they were ready to go. Rex had his gloves and helmet in Clay's van and his bike strapped down in the trailer next to Clay's. Clay punched the address for Eli's cycle shop, and they took the surface roads from Rex to Eli's place. As much as they both loved living in Tucson, the city had very few freeways, meaning that to get across town, you were limited to surface roads. Most of the time, it was cool, but it easily turned what should be a 15-minute drive in any other city of approximately the same size into a 45-minute crawl through local neighborhoods.

They finally made it to Eli's shop. Knowing that the man had died the week beforehand gave the bike shop an eerie feeling. They made some small talk to the two employees who were tasked with selling all of Eli's stock and explained why they were there. The female worker (whose name Rex always forgot) led them through to the back of his workshop and into the alley behind it. She casually pointed to the locked garage behind her and walked back into the shop to carry on with whatever she was working on before they interrupted her.

Rex walked up to the locked gate, holding the padlock in his left hand. He turned to Clay and declared.

'Well, this is it. The moment of truth."

'What do you mean by the moment of truth?" asked Clay, a little bit confused.

"Well, we get to see this precious bike Eli wants us to deliver to his long-lost daughter," Rex sighed. He loved Clay like a brother, but he could be a bit slow on the uptake at times.

Rex fished out the lock-up key from his back pocket. The defining moment. He was keen to see what sort of Chopper Eli would have left for his estranged daughter. He stuck the key in and turned. Nothing. Had he got the wrong lock up? He pulled the key out and slid it in again, this time not exactly all the way in; he twisted the key, and the lock started to turn. Phew!

They pulled on the old and worn gate, and the weather-beaten door swung open. They peered inside. A lot of dust and cop webs. Clay looked at Rex with a face like, "Ok, what now?"

Rex looked for a light switch and finally found one on the left side of the door. Wasn't there some unwritten rule that the light switches were meant to be on the right? Oh well, whatever. He found it now.

The first thing they noticed was an old roller. A paint-stripped frame, a decent triple tree springer front fork, some mid-sized rabbit ear handlebars, a solo seat, and two badly deflated tires. Um, okay...

'That's it? That's what he wants us to give to his daughter? Sheesh," commented Clay. "He didn't even put a motor in it."

"That can't be it," Rex replied. "Let's keep looking."

The pair dragged out crates of parts. Rear fenders, various wheels, a couple of cocktail shaker exhausts, and a stack of brand-new hardtail frames. By the looks of them, they had been stored here since the 80s. Other than the shelving, there wasn't much left in the lock-up but a solitary shape hidden behind a dusty old tarp. Clay looked at Rex and nodded. *Yep, it looked promising.*

Rex grabbed hold of the dirty tarp and pulled it for the big reveal. There she was. It was one of the best-looking choppers Rex had ever seen in his life. This scoot was like a work of art. The best candy apple flake paint job he had ever seen in his life. Some 60s-style buckhorn handlebars. A superb hardtail frame. A decent rake on the front forks, nothing too extreme. Immaculately laced custom wheels and what looked like an S and S custom-built big V twin engine. Taped to the seat was the chopper's pink slip. Clay grabbed it, folded it up, and shoved it into his back pocket.

"WOOOOOW," Clay whistled in admiration. "What a thing of beauty."

Rex had to agree. This thing had to be worth at least $100,000 or more. He recalled a couple of Eli's cycles going to Japanese collectors for an easy $125,000.

'Here, give me a hand rolling it out," Rex gestured.

'Sure, bud, hang on," Clay replied, putting down the crate he had in his hands.

Within 15 minutes, Rex and Clay had the bike out and all of the crates of spare parts neatly put away back in the lock-up. Again, they stopped for a moment to admire the gorgeous bike in front of them.

"You know, I got an idea' Rex said

'What's that? A test ride?" asked Clay eagerly.

"Well, not really, no. I think we take the bike into the shop and have them change the oil and the battery and give it a quick once over," Rex explained. "That way, when we finally give it to Eli's daughter, it will be ready to ride."

Clay thought for a moment, "Yeah, that's good thinking. No telling how long Eli had it stashed back there."

Rex went and spoke to the guy and girl in Eli's shop. He explained their situation, and the two staff members agreed. He told them to come back in an hour. Rex and Clay walked around the neighborhood until they found a coffee shop to chill in while they waited.

While they were waiting, Rex's phone went off. Figuring it was someone from Eli's shop, he answered immediately.

Clay watched as Rex went through a series of "yes, "uh huh," "Oh thanks," "Very cool," and "Okay, will do." Whoever it was on the phone, it seemed to Clay that Rex was doing more listening than talking.

"Everything okay?" Clay asked after Rex hung up.

"Yeah, yeah, it was Spike from the Phoenix chapter," Rex explained. "He heard about Eli. Offers his condolences, says we should come up to Phoenix tonight, and they'll take us for dinner and drinks."

"Can we do that?" asked Clay.

"I don't see why not. You can get to Pine Hollow just as easily from Phoenix than Tucson," Rex reasoned. "We drive up. Have a night with the boys and head off in the morning."

"Okay, cool, be good to see them Phoenix guys again," Clay replied.

Rex looked at the time on his phone. 'Shall we go back to the shop and see if they got her running yet?"

Clay finished the last of his coffee. 'Sure, bro, let's go."

They returned to Eli's shop to find the two staff still working on the bike for his daughter. "10 minutes," the guy shouted at Rex when they returned. They took seats on the couch and flicked through some magazines on the coffee table as they waited.

Finally, the scooter was ready to ride and started 2nd kick on most attempts. *Good enough,* Rex thought to himself.

The shop workers helped Rex and Clay wheel the bike out to Clay's van and trailer and made sure she was all strapped down nice and tight before the duo started their run to Phoenix.

CHAPTER 5

The duo left the surface roads of Tucson and jumped on the Westbound I-10 Freeway. Rex always loved the drive from Tucson to Phoenix; well, to be clear, he preferred the ride on his scoot over a van, but it was still enjoyable. He felt like every mountain range they passed was probably used in some John Wayne western film in the 1950s. If they had not been backdrops to shoot outs with bad guys, the hell they should have been. Absolutely majestic scenery. Even better when Clay drove so he could take all this awesomeness in.

They stopped at a rest area just before the Phoenix Metro so they could hit the John. Rex always liked to stop here before they hit the city. The way he saw it, if you needed to piss, better to do it now, as there was never any guarantee you wouldn't hit bad traffic coming into Phoenix. Nothing worse than being stuck in traffic and needing to find a restroom.

'What should we do about accommodation?" Clay asked Rex as they pulled out of the rest area and back onto the I-10.

"Ah, we can get a motel near the airport pretty easily. That's what we did last time," Rex explained. 'There's a bunch of options around there. We leave the van there and Uber to whatever drinking establishment the guys want to meet us at. Let's face it, we don't want to get a DUI before we get out of town."

"Yeah, I get ya," Clay replied, focussing on the traffic ahead of them, which was now starting to thicken.

It took them an hour to get to downtown. They cruised aimlessly through the streets near the airport, looking for a motel that didn't seem too sketchy.

"What about this one?" asked Clay. "They have a pretty reasonable weekly rate, too."

As a rule, Rex usually avoided Motels with weekly rates as they seemed to be filled with druggy types. But the one Clay had found looked fairly safe, all things considered. He spied a couple of parking spots in clear view of the front office, making the likelihood of someone stealing their bikes way less likely.

"This could work," he replied to Clay.

They went in and scored a room with two beds. Rex slipped the clerk an extra $20 on the promise he would keep an eye on their van and bikes all night long. The man, apparently from Pakistan, Bangladesh, or India (Rex could never tell those 3 apart), seemed an honest enough type of guy. That put Rex at ease with leaving their stuff when they went to meet the boys.

After checking in, Rex texted Phoenix Chapter Spike, telling them where they were staying. He then asked Spike where to meet the boys. Spike texted back, saying they would come and pick him and Clay up and take them to dinner. Saved an Uber ride, at the very least.

Spike and two other Phoenix club members showed up an hour later in Spike's pickup truck. They jumped on a freeway (It might have actually been the I-10 again; Rex couldn't tell) and, after a few miles, pulled off. From what Rex could ascertain, they were somewhere in Uptown Phoenix. Spike had driven them to a family-run, old-school-style Steak house for Prime Rib. It was good. Over food and beers, they traded stories about Eli's life. Rex told the tale of first meeting Eli and the bar fight, which the two bikers with Spike had never heard before. Soon, everyone had tears of laughter as Rex re-told Eli rising up from a sea of bar stools and a table to beat the Hellbound Nomads senseless.

One of Spike's club brothers (Rex couldn't figure out if that was Steve or Tim) told the table a story about drinking with Eli in some dive bar in Mesa, Arizona. They had run out of money but wanted to keep drinking, so while he kept talking to the bartender, Eli would reach around the bar and grab two more beers. They got so drunk that night that he had a hangover for two days. Of course, Eli was fine the next morning.

After consuming the best prime rib Rex had ever eaten and countless beers, it was time for the boys to be taken back to their motel. Spike wished them well on their quest and told them to hit them up next time they were passing through Phoenix. Rex and Clay were drunk but not completely wasted. They waved at the night clerk as they walked past the van and trailer. Everything was all good in the hood.

Rex awoke around 8 am the next morning. He had a hangover but nothing too brutal, which was a miracle considering the amount they all had to drink the night before. His mouth was super dry, and he was in desperate need of hydration. He looked over to see Clay just coming to the bed next to him.

"How ya feeling, bro?" he asked his old friend.

"Like Dog shit, I need coffee, I need water, and I need bacon and eggs," Clay declared.

"Ughh yeah, me too," Rex replied. "I think I am gonna need to eat before I can drive."

Rex got up, hit the bathroom, brushed his teeth, and pulled on his clothes. "I'm going to go and ask the clerk if there is a decent breakfast place within walking distance," he explained to Clay before heading out.

As it happened, there was one 2 blocks away, so when Rex returned to the room, he told Clay to hurry up so they could go eat. That lazy bastard had gone back to bed.

Rex got Clay out of bed and dressed. "Hurry up, man, I don't want to miss breakfast," Rex scolded Clay.

The two trudged up the street following the Motel clerk's directions. Sure enough, two blocks later was a family-owned and operated diner.

The pair grabbed a booth and scoured the menu. Rex liked the idea of the build-your-own breakfast option, and Clay followed suit.

Their waitress came and took their order.

"We need coffee and ice water right away, please," Clay begged her.

She returned with their drinks, and once they were ready, she asked them for their food orders.

"Hmm, I'll have scrambled eggs, hash browns, and bacon, please," asked Rex

She wrote that down and turned to Clay. "And what about you, sir?" she asked.

"Yeah, I'll have 2 eggs, sunny side up, french fries, sourdough toast, and breakfast sausage, please," Clay replied.

"No problem, coming right up," she replied, walking off to take their order.

Clay chugged his ice water and cradled his coffee. "Damn, it was good to see the Phoenix boys last night."

"Yeah, agreed. That's got to be the best prime rib I've had in a long time," Rex added.

A busboy came by and filled their water glasses.

After 5 minutes, their waitress reappeared, serving them their plates. She checked if they needed more coffee and then left them to enjoy their meals.

Clay stared at his plate, momentarily confused.

"Problem?" asked Rex

"Yeahhhh," Clay replied

'What?" asked Rex

'You want those sausages?" asked Clay

Rex looked at his plate. "No, no, you have them."

Clay reached over and plucked the sausages from Rex's plate and put them on his. "Here, have my bacon; I don't like bacon," he said, using his fork to transfer the bacon to Rex's plate.

"Thanks," Rex replied, thinking about the road trip they had to take today.

"Hey, Rex," asked Clay 'You want those fries?"

Rex thought for a moment *Fries? I didn't order fries.* 'Nah, bro, I hate fries for breakfast. You take 'em."

Clay grabbed the fries in his hands and transferred them from Rex's plate to his.

He stared back down at Rex's plate. "Hey, Rex"

'What?" asked Rex

"Can I get that toast? I love sourdough bread," Clay asked.

"What?" asked Rex incredulously. He looked down at his plate and realized what had happened.

"You dumbass," Rex chastised Clay. "She gave us the wrong plates!'

"Oh shit, yeah, you're right!" Clay exclaimed – he proceeded to grab both plates and slide them to opposite sides of the table. 'But now my fries, sausage, and toast are on your plate!"

Rex shook his head. He loved Clay, but he could be mighty dumb at times. He had to pick up the items Clay had transferred to his plate and hand them back yet again.

Luckily, the food was good, and all the grease helped mop up the booze in their systems. Rex felt human again and was now ready to start his day. He waved at the waitress and made the "Check, please" gesture. After paying their tab, he asked Clay if he was ready to leave.

'Yeah, man, I gotta drop a deuce when we get back to the hotel. Other than that, I am golden," Clay replied.

"Ok, let's head back and check out," Rex replied.

As they left the diner, they witnessed a Dodge Charger fly past them at about 65 mph (in a 30 mph zone)

'Damn, that dude is moving out," Clay exclaimed as the car rocketed by.

'Yep," Rex replied.

Moments later, they heard a sickening screech of tires on asphalt, followed by a metal-on-metal crunch.

"Oh shit, oh shit, oh shit," Rex shouted. "That sounds like the motel. Cmon!'

They ran as fast as they could with full breakfast bellies, their coffee and water sloshing about in their guts. Sure enough, they could see smoke coming from the motel car park. *Fuck*!

From the angle they were on, it looked like the dumb prick in the Charger had crashed right into Clay's van and trailer. Rex's first thought was Eli's gift for his daughter.

"Nooo!" he shouted.

By the time they got to their motel, they were greeted by the sight of some lady in her mid-50s arguing with the day clerk. Her crashed Charger wedged in between Clay's van and trailer.

'Who parked their vehicle there?" she screeched at the manager.

"You're drunk!" he shouted back at her.

In the distance, Rex could hear police sirens. For once, they were not the troublemakers. Felt good.

Rex immediately checked the bikes; Clay could see that the right rear wheel of Clay's van was ruined. Ouch, that was gonna cost a lot to repair. Rex looked over the bikes. Thankfully, Eli's masterpiece chopper was still intact. He checked his bike, and yep, it was all good. Clay's bike, though, nope, the front wheel was destroyed. Major bummer.

As the woman and the motel clerk argued, several of the guests came out of their rooms to check out the drama.

The police finally arrived. Parking in the middle of the entrance to the motel courtyard effectively blocks anyone from entering or leaving.

The first thing they did was separate the drunken woman and the day clerk at their motel.

From what Rex could tell, they were doing the ol' 'She said / He said," and the cops were getting both sides of the story. Clay pushed through the crowd of spectators and started shouting at the woman, "You wrecked my bike, you wrecked my van, you're gonna pay."

Rex went up to support his friend. Before he knew it, he and Clay were being thrown to the ground at gunpoint and being handcuffed by two new cops.

"WHAT THE HELL. Get off me," hollered Clay

They were dragged to the curb further into the motel carpark and told to sit.

One cop stood over them, his gun now holstered, while the heavy-handed cop went back and spoke with the others.

'This is bullshit," Clay swore. "That stupid bitch wrecked my van and scooted."

'Yeah, I know, bro," Clay replied. "Just be calm, and we will get this resolved."

"Fuck!" swore Clay.

One of the original cops came up to them and started questioning them. Who were they? Why were they here? Where were they headed?

Rex didn't feel they needed to know they were heading North and just explained to the cop that they were up from Tucson visiting friends. Why give law enforcement any more info than they deserve? Let them figure that out amongst themselves.

"Ughh, I gotta take a shit," Clay complained.

"Tell the cop, not me," Rex snipped.

"Hey, I need to hit the bathroom," Clay shouted at the cop who was tasked to "keep an eye on them."

"Just hold it in," the officer shouted back. "You two are not going anywhere until this is all cleared up."

"Oh, come on," Clay shouted back at the cop in frustration.

The two bikers sat on the curb in the motel courtyard for another 30 minutes as the cops came back time and time again, asking the same questions over and over, hoping to try and catch them in a lie. Eventually, they figured out that Rex and Clay really were the victims here, and they un-cuffed them both. Clay hit the bathroom in the motel while Rex stood outside talking to the cop. The cop explained that the lady was going to jail on suspicion of drunk driving and that Clay should file a claim with his insurance company, for which the cop would vouch. Rex was relieved it was finally resolved, but he could have done it without being handcuffed and treated like a felon when they hadn't done anything wrong. Same ol' same ol', the cops would never learn.

After Clay returned from taking a massive dump, they tried to figure out their next steps. Rex suggested he ride Eli's chopper, and Clay could ride his Harley. Clay argued he should get to ride it since he was the one who lost his bike in the accident. In the end, Rex resigned himself to riding his own bike, and Clay rode the custom scoot. Clay made a fair argument, and Rex could admit to himself (never to Clay, though) that he was kinda jealous. After figuring all that out, they decided to speak to the motel clerk. He advised them that they couldn't leave the van and trailer there despite it not being their fault.

Frustrated, Rex called Spike, the Phoenix Chapter president, and asked for help. As it happens, one of the Phoenix boys owned an auto shop and would send an employee with a tow truck to collect Clay's van and trailer for them. After speaking with the auto shop owner, Spike called Rex back and told them they could leave it at the shop for as long as they needed. The second problem was solved.

The day clerk did agree not to throw the boys out of their room past check out as they waited for Spike's buddy to come and collect the van. 45 minutes later, he arrived. They spent 5 minutes figuring out what they could pack with them. Limited by what they could bungee cord it to their scoots and said their goodbyes to Clay's battered van and trailer.

Finally, after many wasted hours, it was time to get back on the road again.

CHAPTER 6

"I'm so glad we had Eli's people change out the oil and battery on that beauty, eh?" Rex asked Clay

"Oh yeah, we would have been screwed otherwise," Clay replied, sitting on Eli's masterpiece and coming to grips with the stance of the bike.

'Whatever you do, don't wreck it," teased Rex

"Fuck you," Clay laughed.

Rex checked his GPS – from what he could tell – they had to take the 87 Freeway North, turn on to the 260, and then grab the 77 North after Show Low. All in all, it was a little over 3 hours. Factor in stopping every hundred miles for gas; due to Eli's chopper having a peanut tank, they should make it just before 6 PM. Doable. However, his GPS was sending them out via Globe. This had happened before where, logically, he knew the way to go someplace, and the GPS told him to take an alternative route. Usually, he would ignore it only to see the GPS was right and he was wrong (Road works, traffic accidents, etc), so this time, he figured they would take no chances.

They found the 60 heading east and merged onto the highway. Traffic wasn't too bad yet, but Rex was worried Clay would do something stupid, and they would trash Eli's gift for his estranged daughter.

They made it to the Globe Miami area, stopped at a Circle K, gassed up, hit the restroom, and bought some snacks to munch on.

"You know, I just thought of something," Clay announced, finishing off a bag of taco chips.

'What's that, brother?" asked Rex

"Well, once we get to Pine Hollow and give this scoot to Eli's daughter Samantha, how the hell am I getting home?"

Rex thought for a moment. "Hmm, good question. I'll have Spike's guys work on your van, and maybe they can bring it up to us."

"Oh yeah, that sounds good," Clay replied

"Or we could ride nuts to butts back down to Phoenix to collect it," Rex laughed.

"Yeah, I guess," said Clay, not really finding the funny side of it.

Once they passed Globe, the highway really opened up for them, and the high desert views they had were simply breathtaking. It made Rex proud to be from Arizona. You just didn't get views like this back East. Then came the scenic twists and turns of the Salt River Canyon. Rex was in biker heaven. He kept one eye on Clay, hoping he wouldn't blow it on Eli's chopper.

After 3 hrs of riding, they passed through the town of Show Low, which was beautiful. In an ideal world, Rex could see himself owning a summer house up here to escape the brutal heat of Tucson and Phoenix.

15 minutes after Show Low, they were seeing signs for Pine Hollow. Rex marveled at how they were still in the same state as the scenery and the plants, and everything was so different from

33

what you usually expected from Arizona. He could understand the appeal.

As they slowed down heading into town, Rex noticed the 'Welcome to Pine Hollow sign," population 9000. It should be fairly easy to find Eli's daughter, Samatha, here. After all, in small-town living, everyone knows everyone. Usually, their personal business, too.

As they rolled into town, Rex kept his eyes open for a motel. He assumed that towns like this made most of their money from tourism, so there had to be at least a couple of motels to choose from. They spotted one with a vacancy sign illuminated and pulled in. Clay waited outside while Rex went in to ask about the rates. Being reasonable, he booked one room with two beds for the night. After checking in and dumping their bags, they pondered their next moves.

'I think we should go and find Samantha right away," Rex stated 'Let's gift her Eli's bike, eat some food, maybe have a couple of drinks, and head back to Phoenix in the morning."

Clay thought for a moment. "Ok, sounds good. How do we find her?"

"Eli gave me an address. I'll put it in my GPS app, and we can get to her before nightfall. Easy Peasy," Rex replied.

'Let's go then," Clay replied, jumping up and grabbing his riding gear.

CHAPTER 7

Rex's GPS led them down through the main street and out of town. There were houses here, but most were fairly spread apart from each other. He followed the app's directions, which had them turning right off the main road and going further into the hills. A quick left after that, and they were on Samantha's street. Great, they would be there in 3 minutes. Knock on the door and explain who they were. Gift her the bike and be back in town in 10 minutes.

Samantha's street kept going and going; there were fewer and fewer houses now and further and further spread out. Geez, where was her place? Finally, the GPS told Rex that it was near the next bend on the road. To his dismay, as they turned the corner, there was nothing there but the burnt-out shell of a house. With weeds growing everywhere, it seemed this house hadn't been used any time in recent years. *Fuck, now what?*

"Why are we stopping here? Clay asked.

"Well, believe it or not. This is where she was meant to have been living. Dammit," Rex replied.

"Oh shit, we're screwed. Does this mean I get to keep the bike?" asked Clay.

"Haha, nice try, no it does not," Rex replied 'Someone in town will know where she is. I say we head back and ask around."

"Okay, so what do you suggest?" asked Clay

Rex thought for a moment. "Alright, how about this? We ride back to the main street – you take one side of the street, I'll take the other, we stop in on every business and ask about Samantha McCallum."

"Okay," Clay replied.

"Small towns like this," Rex continued. "Everyone knows everyone else's business. I guarantee that if she is still in town, someone will know where she is. But, if she left town, someone would have a rough idea at least of where she went."

"Makes sense," Clay replied.

They fired up their rides, swung them around, and headed back into town. Rex waved and signaled Clay to pull over once they went to the edge of Main Street.

Rex pointed up the street. "Okay, How about this? I'll ride up to the far end of town; you know where we came in off the highway."

"Okay," Clay replied.

"I'll then turn around, work my way back, and you start on this side of town, and I'll guess we will meet up in the middle," Rex suggested.

Clay thought about the pros and cons of riding up and back. He was about to say something when he noticed a dive bar 4 doors down from where they had parked.

'Sure!" I'll take this side. Meet you in a few," Clay replied.

CHAPTER 8

Clay parked Eli's award-winning scoot and left his helmet balanced on the ape hangers. He tucked his riding gloves into his back pocket and started down the block, watching Rex ride off into the distance.

The first storefront he came to was an antique store. He tried the door handle, locked. Oh well, on to the next store. This was a touristy gift shop and again locked. Clay looked at his phone. It was just after 5 PM. What was wrong with these people? Closing at 5 PM? Weird.

The next place was a little laundromat. The only person in attendance was an elderly Hispanic woman. The problem was she couldn't speak any English, and Clay didn't speak any Spanish. After a couple of half-hearted attempts to make a conversation with her, Clay gave up and left the place.

Then came the dive bar. The Dead Crow Saloon. Clay decided he liked the place based on the name alone.

He walked into the dimly lit bar. Loud hard rock blared out over the jukebox; it sounded like that band Buckcherry, which Clay had seen a Sturgis a few years back. *Well, alright!* He thought to himself. A couple of patrons sat in various booths, and Clay made a beeline for the bar, sitting down in front of the somewhat attractive 40-something barmaid.

"Modello, please?" he asked. "With a slice of lime, thanks"

The barmaid held up three fingers. *$3 for a beer?* I thought, Clay Wow, that *I can see the appeal of this town.*

He pulled $5 out of his wallet and handed it to her. She quickly returned and left him two singles as change.

"New in town?' she asked.

"Yeah. From Tucson," Clay replied

"So what brings you to our little town?" she shouted over the ear-splitting hard rock music...

"I'm looking for someone," Clay replied. "A woman named Samantha, you know her?"

"Yeah!" she replied.

"Oh, no shit," Clay replied. *He couldn't believe his luck; the first person he ran into and knew was Samantha McCallum!*

'Yeah," she replied with a knowing smile.

"Wait, you're Samantha?" he shouted back over the ear-splitting music.

"Yeah, Samantha," the woman nodded.

Rex was going to be so pleased. He had found Samantha immediately. He could give her the bike now. He and Rex could grab some food, maybe a few beers, and ride back to Phoenix tomorrow. The Quest for Eli's bike for his long-lost daughter was over.

"I want to give you something," he shouted over the next band, which sounded a lot like Slayer.

"What?" she asked

'I want to give you something," Clay repeated.

'What???" she shouted back.

He started to act out what he was trying to say to her using hand gestures, but it just turned out wrong. Him pointed at himself and then pointed at her.

Then, it occurred to Clay. *I have the pink slip. If I show her that, she will get what I mean right away.*

He held up his hand in a "hold on" type gesture. Samantha was confused.

He reached into his back pocket and pulled out the pink slip. He pointed at himself, then at her. She was still confused. Then he held up the pink slip, gesturing to her to take it. She stepped back a moment at first, a little confused as to what he wanted from her.

He then made the sign your name hand gesture. Her facial expression was one of "ahhh." She reached onto the bar counter and grabbed a pen. He repeated the 'sign your name" gesture and thrust the pink slip into her face.

She looked up at Clay with a face like *Really? Do you really want me to sign this?*

Clay nodded enthusiastically.

Samantha signed it. A long flowing squiggle of a signature like a movie star might do. Clay nodded and smiled at her. She blushed. She thought for a moment like she wanted to say something, thought better of it. Turning back, I grabbed a bottle of whiskey off the shelf and two shot glasses. She poured two shots and returned the bottle. Passing one of the shot glasses to Clay, she chinked them together and took a shot. Clay followed her lead and did his shot. Felt that old familiar kick to the chest as he downed the brown liquor.

After Clay had finished his beer, he gestured for Samantha to come outside with him. At first, she shook her head, indicating that she had a bar to tend to. Clay shook his head and gave her a "Come on" gesture with his hand. She finally relented, shrugged and slipped out from behind the bar to follow Clay outside.

Stepping out into the early evening air, Clay turned to Samantha, "I can't believe I found you," he declared.

'I can't believe I found YOU," she replied, which Clay thought was weird as he wasn't aware she was looking for him.

"There she is," he pointed at the Award-winning Chopper, "She's all yours. Let me grab my helmet."

'Really? I can really have it?" she asked. "Are you sure?"

'Yes, of course! It's all yours!" Clay replied happily.

"Oh my god, you're the best," she replied, violently hugging him.

He handed her the keys. She hugged him again. He finally managed to break free, and he said goodbye to her. Rex was gonna be so pleased when he found out their mission was over.

He said his goodbyes to Samantha and, with his helmet, walked off up Main Street in search of Rex.

CHAPTER 9

The main street in Pine Hollow seemed to be about 9-10 blocks long. If he crossed over to the other side of the street and walked up, Clay was confident he would find Rex in the next 15 minutes. Too easy.

He peered in the storefronts of the shops as he continued working his way back toward the direction of their motel. Seemed like a cool little town to retire or even vacation in. Clay could see the appeal.

A couple more blocks and no sign of Rex. He had to be here somewhere. The next block Clay approached seemed to consist of bars and restaurants. For these, he actually spent time walking into each one and making sure Rex wasn't having a sneaky beer or eating dinner without him. He got a few suspicious looks from the locals but shrugged it off, and he was used to getting the evil eye from strangers, came with the patch. No big deal.

Still no Rex. He continued up the main street. Another block, a hardware store, a book shop and a supermarket all closed for the evening. Clay peered ahead and thought he spotted Rex's Harley parked 2 blocks up. Good. He would skip ahead and hopefully find him on the block where his bike was parked.

The first spot Clay came to on the block with Rex's scoot was a breakfast place, clearly closed for the evening. A couple of gift shops and another dive bar. He contemplated hitting the dive bar but didn't want to get distracted in case he missed Rex. Just as he was about to walk past the bar, the door flung open, and there was Rex.

Hey!" Rex said in surprise, not expecting to see Clay.

"Hey, brother. Do I have news for you!" Clay smiled.

"Well, I got news for you; wait for you to hear what I found out," exclaimed Rex, all excited.

"Uh.." said Clay, itching to tell Rex the good news.

"So I got news on Samantha," Rex added excitedly, not giving Clay time to speak.

"Her biological mother died 15 years ago, but her best friend Nina became Samantha's legal guardian." Rex continued."Samantha is here in town and works at the local supermarket!"

"Ah, cool, but..." Clay tried to interject.

'Their house burnt down some time back, but they live off the main street like 2 miles from here!" Rex explained. 'Yeah, so we are making headway. Oh, what's your news?"

"Ahh, yeah, well." Clay started, "I met Samantha at a Dive Bar at the other end of Main Street and already gave her the Chopper!"

"What?" asked Rex, completely blindsided by this revelation.

"Yeah, she was working at some bar called the Dead Crow Saloon," explained Clay, "She was older than I expected, though."

'Wait, back up," Rex replied with concern, "Apparently, Samantha is 24 or 25. How old was this chick at the bar?"

"Hmm, at a guess 40?" Clay replied, "Hard to tell; the bar was pretty dimly lit."

Rex swore under his breath, "Clay, where's Eli's bike?"

"Oh, I gave it to her already; she signed the pink slip and everything. We can head back to Phoenix in the morning."

Rex felt sick, "Bro, how do you know that was Samantha?"

"Oh, I asked her. And she said yes," Clay explained, all pleased with himself.

"Did you ask for I.D. or anything?" Rex asked.

'I.d.? That would have been rude, don't you think?" Clay replied, somewhat confused.

Rex was really worried now. "Dude, take me back to this bar now!"

"Sure, is there a problem?" asked Clay

"Well, shit, I think there might be. We need to get back to this bar asap!" Rex snapped, "Lead the way!"

CHAPTER 10

The pair walked the blocks back to the Dead Crow. Clay held the door open for Rex, and they both filed in.

"Point her out, bro," Rex asked of Clay.

Clay looked around the dingy bar but couldn't see her. There was a dude behind the bar now. He looked like one of those college hippy kids who smoked a little weed, dropped some acid, and went and saw Dead and Co. and Dark Star Orchestra every time they played Flagstaff.

Clay walked up to him with Rex following.

"Hey, you," Clay shouted over the music 'Where's Samantha?" he asked.

"Who?" the hippy kid replied.

"Samantha, the bartender!" Clay replied.

"No one called Samantha works here, bro," the Hippy kid replied.

"I was in here an hour ago; there was some chick working here," Clay explained.

"Oh, you mean Nina?" the hippy kid replied.

"Who?" asked Clay.

"The bartender," the Hippy Kid replied.

"Ah, okay, Nina. Is she coming back?" Clay asked the Hippie Kid.

The hippy kid thought about it for a moment. "Yeah, she had to run out to do some errands or something. She should be back in an hour if ya wanna wait."

Clay shouted to Rex, "She's back in 1 hour, wanna grab a beer?"

Rex agreed, and they ordered two beers and two shots.

Clay and Rex grabbed seats by the bar and just chilled, waiting for Samantha / Nina to return. Clay figured that maybe Nina was a name she gave the bar owner to avoid taxes or something. He was confident this would all get resolved in the next hour.

90 minutes passed, and there was still no sign of Samantha / Nina. Clay grabbed the hippy kid.

"Hey man, where is she? You told us one hour!" Clay hissed.

The hippy kid looked like he was about to shit himself.

'Whoa, chill man, chill. Let me text her," he replied.

He grabbed his phone and started madly typing. A few minutes later, he returned to Clay.

"She'll be back in 5 minutes she says," holding his phone in front of Clay's face as proof.

The hippy kid handed them two more beers, "On the house," he shouted over the loud music.

Clay sipped his beer, keeping one eye on the front door so that Samantha could return. Finally, she came in through a rear staff entrance. He nodded at her as she went behind the bar. She looked at him like she had seen a ghost. She was spooked.

Clay nudged Rex, "That's her."

The look on Rex's face was one of controlled rage. As far as she was concerned, there was no way this "Samantha."

He waved her over.

"You need to step outside with us NOW," he shouted.

The look of fear on her face was palpable.

CHAPTER 11

She stared at Rex and then at Clay. She shook her head, almost as if she was in disgust. She said something to Hippy Kid, which Clay couldn't hear, and then motioned for them to follow her out the back of the dive bar.

She leads them out a narrow back door into a darkened car park. No sooner were they out of the head-pounding rock music from the bar Rex grabbed the barmaid.

'What's your name? You're not Samantha!" he shouted.

'Woah woah, easy there, killer. I never said my name was Samantha," she corrected him.

Rex scowled and looked over at Clay. "He says you told him your name was Samantha!"

'I never told him that. I thought he asked if I knew Samantha!" she snapped at Rex. "I'm her legal guardian! My name is Nina."

Rex shot Clay a dagger stare. 'Where's that chopper?" he asked.

Nina looked worried.

'He gave it to me!" she pointed at Clay.

"Yeah, I know that," Rex snapped, "He told me he gave it to you because he thought you were Samantha."

"I never said I was Samantha," Nina protested, "He gave it to me; it was mine to do what I please with."

'Whaaaaa," Rex rolled his eyes 'What have you done?"

Nina paused for a minute and then said, almost under her breath, "I sold it to a friend."

CHAPTER 12

Rex swore under his breath, 'Well, go buy it back, and we can forget this whole misunderstanding."

Nina groaned, "Ah, it's not that simple. I owed him money. I traded the motorcycle to pay off my debts."

Rex swore again under his breath. Between Clay's foolish mistakes and this woman, he was going to blow a gasket.

"I'm sure if we went and visited your friend, we could work this all out," suggested Clay.

"I'm not so sure he will be open to that," Nina replied

"Well, we gotta at least try," Clay replied, "Right, Rex?'

Rex shook his head. He could barely contain his rage. "How far is this friend of yours?"

"He's a few blocks from here, walking distance," Nina replied.

'Well, show us the way," Rex insisted.

"Well, it's not that easy; I have a bar to tend to," Nina protested.

"Wait here," Rex insisted. He walked back into the bar and right up to Hippy College kid.

"Nina has to step out again. She is helping us with a problem. You're okay with that, right?"

The hippy kid looked petrified. "Uhhhh , yes?" he stammered.

"I figured as much. She will be back soon enough," Rex said, turning and walking back outside again.

"Okay, your co-worker is all right with you cutting out again. Show us the way to your friend's place," Rex said.

"He did? Um, ok, follow me," Nina said, walking away from the bar.

Rex and Clay followed the 40-something Nina down the alley that ran parallel to Main Street.

The trio walked what Rex assumed was South for a couple of blocks before they came to a run-down warehouse.

'Wait here," Nina instructed them, leaving them about 15 feet from the side door. Rex noticed a video camera aimed at the door.

Nina banged on the door and announced, "It's me again. Nina,"

Rex heard the door buzzing, signaling that someone had unlocked it.

Nina held the door open and looked back at the two bikers. "Well, cmon then," she said.

Rex and Clay followed the barmaid into the warehouse.

CHAPTER 13

"What do you want?" a voice came from somewhere deep in the warehouse.

"Uh, my friends need to speak with you," explained Nina

Rex and Clay followed Nina to the far side of the run-down building. A section that had been converted into a couple of separate offices.

Two big cowboys stepped out of the shadows and put their hands on both Rex and Clay's chests.

"Hold on there, fellas, gotta give you a pat down," explained the one in the red flannel shirt.

Rex sighed and held up his arms to let the redneck check him for weapons. Usually, he didn't leave home without his everyday carry pistol but had chosen to leave it back in Tucson this trip. He was beginning to wish he had taken it with him.

Reassured that neither Rex nor Clay were armed, the cowboys let them continue into the office part of their warehouse.

"Bikers, eh?" said the man sitting behind the desk, "Two percenters at that."

"One percenter," Clay corrected him, "Two percent is like fat-free milk or something."

"Yeah, whatever," the man sitting down said dismissively.

'So what's your problem? What can I do for you?" the man asked.

Rex decided he didn't like this guy. They would just collect the bike for Samantha and leave.

"Hey, I'm Rex, and this is my buddy Clay," Rex introduced himself and held out his hand, "Who do I have the pleasure of talking to?"

The cowboy stood up, "Hey Rex, I'm Dan. Dan Thatcher, nice to meet ya," he shook Rex's hand and then nodded at Clay.

'There's been a misunderstanding with Nina, and we are here to clear things up," Rex explained.

"There's no misunderstanding from my side," Dan replied. "Not sure what business you have with her, but it's nothing to do with me."

'Well, you see," Rex explained, "My friend Clay here gave a motorcycle to Nina, thinking she was someone else. We are here to collect it."

'Gave her a motorcycle?" Dan exclaimed, "That's mighty generous of you."

"Yeah, so if you can just give it back to us, we can be on our way," Rex replied.

"Whoa, whoa. Do you have the pink slip?" asked Dan.

Rex looked over at Clay, and he shook his head sheepishly.

"No? No?" Rex asked of Clay, again incredulous.

"Well, Mister Clay," Dan started

"No, no, I am Rex, he is Clay," Rex corrected, pointing at Clay.

"Well, Mister Rex," said Dan, "I happen to have a legal pink slip for a nice-looking chopper in my possession," Dan smiled at the two bikers.

'Yeah, well, that's ours," Clay interrupted.

"No, it's mine," Dan corrected him, "I would be happy to sell it to you if you were interested in buying it from me."

'Fuck," Rex swore.

"Hey now, no need for profanity," Dan smiled.

'Are you interested or not?" he asked them.

"Look, man, I'm sure you are the king of this town or something, but we just want our bike back," Rex replied, exasperated by the whole evening's events.

"As I said, I would be happy to sell it back to you," Dan smiled, "The way I see it, a motorcycle like that would be fairly expensive."

"Uh huh," Rex replied, knowing where this was going. "What price are we talking about here?"

"Well, like I was saying, I reckon a bike like that would be fairly expensive, say.... $3500? $3000?"

Rex couldn't believe it. This redneck had no idea what he had on his hands.

"It's worth..." Clay started to say, but Rex managed to nudge his boot on his own to shut him up.

"$3000 seems fair," Rex replied, "Only one problem: we don't have the cash right now."

"Well, I can't just give you the bike on a promise you will pay me down the road," Dan replied, "This isn't a charity here."

"Can I have a quick word in private with my buddy here?" Rex asked Dan.

'Sure, just step outside; my guys can let you back in when you're done," Dan replied.

'C'mon Clay," said Rex, "Let's step outside for a minute."

The two bikers turned and exited the warehouse the way they had come in.

CHAPTER 14

"What do you reckon?" asked Rex to Clay once they were outside.

"That guy is a fool. He had seriously undervalued that Chopper," Clay replied.

'Yes, but don't you see? That's a good thing. We never want him to find out the real value of that bike," Rex explained.

"Ahh yeah, I didn't think of that," Clay replied. "Good thinking"

Rex rolled his eyes.

"Let me make a quick call to the Phoenix boys. See if they have $3000 they can lend us," Rex explained.

Rex called a few of the boys. Unfortunately, no one has any spare cash at this time.

Fuck, we made a vow to Eli we can't let him down. Rex thought.

"There's gotta be a way to figure this out with these cowboys," Rex said to Clay 'We can't let down Eli."

"I know!" exclaimed Clay, "We say we want it, but we need a day or two to get the cash together. Then we return late tonight, break in and steal it!"

Rex thought for a moment, actually considering it.

"Nah, nah, that won't work," Rex replied, " We steal it, gift it to Eli's daughter and then Dan and his wannabe thugs see Samantha riding it around town? They will probably hurt her. We can't do that."

"Shit yeah, you're right," Clay replied. "Well, I dunno then, I am out of ideas."

"All I know is we got to get him to agree to this price, and then we can figure it out from there," Rex replied, "Let's head back in. Maybe there is some construction work or something we can do around here to raise the money?"

"Yeah, okay, let's head back in," Clay replied.

Rex buzzed them, and one of Dan's goons let them back into the fortified warehouse. Rex pushed past the redneck and made his way back to Dan's office. He sat back down in the chair opposite Dan's desk.

"Okay, so, here's the deal," Rex started 'We do want the bike. $3000's fair, but we don't have the money right now. Do you know if anyone is hiring around town? Construction work or anything?"

Dan thought for a moment. "Not that I can think of," he paused. "However, I might have some work for ya."

Rex wasn't sure he liked where this was heading. 'Oh yeah? What sort of work would that be?"

"You boys look like you can handle yourselves," Dan started.

"You know we can," Clay interrupted.

"So I do have some security work. You boys do that for me, and I will trade you the bike. Fair?" Dan asked.

Rex thought for a moment. He leaned over Dan's desk with his hand out to shake. "Ok, deal."

Rex and Dan shook on it.

'Gimme your number, and I'll text you tomorrow," said Dan, "I assume you're staying in town?"

Rex gave Dan his cell phone number, "Yeah, some motel just on the outskirts of the main street."

"Okay, cool, I'll be in touch," Dan said, dismissing the two bikers.

CHAPTER 15

R ex and Clay trudged down a side street to rejoin the main road. They figured they would walk up, collect Rex's bike, take it back to the hotel, and then get something to eat.

By the time they took Rex's chopper back to their motel and walked back onto Main Street, pretty much everything was closed.

"Damn, I'm starving," Clay complained.

"There has to be something open in this one-horse town," Rex replied. "Shit, at this point, I would even settle for a couple of gas station hot dogs."

"Ugh, gross. 0/10 I would not recommend," Clay replied.

"The voice of experience, eh?" teased Rex.

'Oh, you know it," Clay laughed, "I'll tell you over some beers sometime."

A pickup truck rolled by, heading out of town. Rex kinda wished they were on their way out of town, too. But a promise is a promise, especially to a dead man. There was no way to back out of their pledge now.

Rex looked both ways on the deserted Main Street of Pine Hollow. He then stepped out into the middle of the road and looked as far down the road as he could see.

"Okay, well, there is some neon signage up ahead on the right about 2 blocks down and possibly something on the left side of the street about 5 blocks away. I say we try the place on the right, and if that isn't open, we can wander down to the lights on the left side of the road," Rex explained.

"Okay, sounds like a plan," Clay replied, "I guess if nothing opens, we starve tonight."

"There's got to be a vending machine back at the motel – we should be able to grab some potato chips if nothing else," Rex suggested.

The pair walked down Main Street in silence. Sure, it was weird being in a town that closed at sunset. Rex figured. There were probably similar small towns all over the USA, much like Pine Hollow.

The pair made it to the well-illuminated neon Rex, which had spotted two blocks back. A hardware store. Who would pay to have a hardware store lit up all night? Made zero sense to Rex, but what did he know about small-town living? They only had one option left now: to cross the street and head to where Rex thought there were some other storefronts lit up.

'So what should we do about Samantha?" asked Clay

'What do you mean, bro?" asked Rex.

'I mean, should we reach out and let her know we are in town or something?" Clay explained.

"Ahh, hmm, good question," Rex replied, "I guess we should wait until we get that Chopper back from those rednecks then we reach out?"

"Yeah, I guess," Clay replied.

They continued down the Northbound side of Main Street.

'Are you kidding me?" Rex said out loud

"What? What's the problem?" asked Clay

"It's that dive bar again, The Dead Crow," Rex explained. 'Hopefully, the kitchen is still open"

The bikers entered the bar, and Hippy Kid and Nina looked up as they crossed the room. Both had looked close to sheer panic in their faces.

Rex and Clay grabbed seats by the bar.

"We need food," Rex explained.

"Can't you eat elsewhere?" asked Nina somewhat rudely.

"Nothing else is open in your small town," Clay explained.

Nina went off and spoke to the hippy kid.

"Okay, we can do burgers and fries, but that's it," Nina told them both.

"Fine," Rex replied, "And two beers, please."

The hippy kid went back to the kitchen to work on the food. Nina reached down and grabbed two bottles of beer for Rex and Clay.

"That hippy kid better not put any drugs in our food," Rex joked.

"Really?" Nina looked at him with a filthy stare. 'I thought all you bikers were into sex, drugs and rock n roll?"

"Nah, just booze for me," Rex explained.

"Oh, what? Your gang doesn't permit it?" Nina snipped.

"Gang? No, we are a club. Big difference," Clay explained.

"Uh huh," Nina replied, "I believe you, millions would not."

"Good for you," Rex replied, not appreciating her sass. 'At least you bothered to turn the music down."

"It's late. We can't have it on too loud after 10 on weeknights," Nina explained, "Small town and all that."

"Cool, I like it when the music is turned down better. I can't hear myself think otherwise," Clay interjected.

The hippy kid returned with burgers and fries for Clay and Rex, and to be honest, it actually looked pretty decent. Then again, maybe Clay was just super hungry.

"Thanks, bro," Clay said as Hippy Kid bought them a tray of condiments to put on their burgers and fries.

Clay bit into his burger, "MMM, not bad," he gave Nina and Hippy Kid a thumbs up.

Rex had to admit that after eating his dinner, he felt a little more optimistic. They would do this "security work" for Dan, get the bike back, track down Samantha and be on their way. They should be on their way home in the next 48 hrs. That would also give the Phoenix boys time to get Clay's van fixed so he could get back to Tucson. Riding nuts to butts was okay in the city, hopping from bar to bar but long-distance riding? Not so much.

"So what's up with this Dan character?" Rex asked Nina after the Hippy kid had gone back to the kitchen to clean the dishes.

"Ughh, where do I start?" Nina groaned at the thought of the guy.

"I dunno? At the beginning? Why do you owe him money?" asked Rex

Nina looked around to make sure no one else was in earshot, "Ugh, drugs," she admitted some, what embarrassed.

'What? Like Coke? Meth?" Rex asked.

"Nah, Oxys, actually," Nina replied.

"What? He sells people Oxygen?" asked Clay

"No, dumbass!" Rex snapped at his brother, "Oxycontin, painkillers."

"Oh shit," said Clay.

"Yeah, Dan thinks he's Mister Big Shot. He pretty much supplies all the towns up here," Nina explained, "All the way up and down Highway 77."

"Hmm. Can't the sheriff shut him down or something?" asked Rex.

'Are you kidding me? The Sheriff is his brother!" said Nina.

"Oh shit," said Rex, "No wonder Dan felt like he was above the law."

"So yeah, I had a pill problem for a while, got in debt to Dan and his pals," Nina told Rex and Clay, "I am not proud of it, but I don't mess with that crap anymore."

"Ok, good," Rex replied, "But why did you say you were Samantha to poor old Clay?"

'Oh, I'm her mother," Nina replied.

Rex's jaw nearly hit the floor. No fucking way. 'What? You?" asked Rex.

'Well, not her real mom. I'm her legal guardian. Her mom died about 15 years ago. Her dying wish was for me to take care of her until she was old enough," said Nina.

Oh fuck, this just gets weirder and weirder, Rex thought to himself.

Nina turned out to be right after all by Rex's reckoning. Clay and Rex stayed at the bar until closing time and walked back with Nina, whose house was off Main Street in the same direction as their motel. They walked back with her about the deserted main road until it was time for her to turn off, and they all said their goodbyes. Rex stood and watched her go, and then they continued on to their motel.

CHAPTER 16

Rex woke the next morning with a slight hangover; all in all, yesterday had been an interesting day.

The first thing he did was text Spike back in Phoenix and find out the latest on Clay's van. Turns out the reach axle was ruined and would need to be replaced. Rex instructed Spike's boys to proceed, but he had no idea how he and Clay were going to be able to afford it.

When Clay finally woke up, he waited for him to take a piss and brush his teeth. Once Clay was ready, they walked down Main Street to look for breakfast. Like the polar opposite of walking back after the dive bar, the street was bustling with people and cars. *What a difference eight hours make,* thought Rex to himself. As they walked down Main Street, some of the locals gave them suspicious glances. Rex couldn't tell if it was because they were outlaw bikers or the fact the locals probably did that to anyone they did not know.

They found a decent-looking breakfast spot and filed in. After being seated at a booth, they checked out the menu. Wow, bacon, eggs, hash browns and toast for $3.50? Not bad!

After they finished eating, Rex nursed his cup of coffee; his hangover was already lifting. He was glad; he was in no mood to spend the day feeling like shit.

"So what do you wanna do today?" Clay asked Rex after paying the check at the diner.

"Eh, we can either take a walk up and down Main Street or go back to the motel and watch TV," Rex suggested.

Clay thought for a moment. "Fuck it, let's just go watch TV. Not much to see in this one-horse town."

"Yeah, works for me," Rex replied.

"I wonder when we will hear from that creep, Dan?" asked Clay.

"Well, he said it sometime today, but who knows? I say today we wait, and if nothing comes up, we drop by and see him Thursday. What do you think?" Rex replied.

"Sounds good, bro," Clay replied

"Hey, I saw a supermarket down here last night; let's go grab some beers for the room," said Rex.

They walked back down Main Street away from their motel to where they remembered the Supermarket being located. On top of grabbing a six-pack each, Clay grabbed them both bags of potato chips. Rex grabbed a banana, too, "For Health reasons," he explained to Clay as they lined up by the cash registers.

Rex noticed a young lady working the register two down from their register, rocking a t-shirt by the band Slipknot. Rex wondered if that was Eli's daughter, Samantha.

As they walked back to their hotel with their "supplies," a could of old geezers going the other way said, "Good morning," to them and tipped their hats. Rex was pleased to see not everyone in this podunk town was so snobbish.

The pair spent the early afternoon watching re-runs of 90s comedy shows and TV and sipping beers. Around 3 PM, Rex heard his phone ping.

It was from an unknown number, and the message simply read, "Be here at 5 PM," Had to be Dan.

'We're on for 5 PM," Rex told Clay.

"Ok, good. I was starting to get bored," Clay replied, "I wonder what this, "security detail," means."

"Probably guarding his stupid warehouse or something," shrugged Rex, "I guess we will see in a couple of hours."

CHAPTER 17

"Okay, so here's the deal," Dan explained, "Every week, my boys drive to Vegas and pick up, uh, "supplies," I need you two to ride with them as security so they don't get ripped off."

"Okay," said Rex.

"I'm thinking one of you ride ahead on your motorcycle and report back to the van on road conditions," Dan continued.

'Well, that would be me," Rex explained, "Clay doesn't have his bike at the moment."

"Okay, so you ride ahead, make sure there's no cops or suspicious characters lying in wait, and report back to your buddy Clay and my guy Cody," said Dan, nodding to one of his henchmen who stood behind Rex and Clay in Dan's office. Rex turned and nodded, "How do you do," to Cody. Cody didn't acknowledge the gesture.

"I can do that," Rex replied. 'So we ride out to Vegas, we do a pickup, and bring it back here, yeah?"

"Pretty much. It's about a 6-hour drive one way, so I would want you guys on the road by 7 am tomorrow, cool?" asked Dan

Rex thought about it for a moment. Up early, on the road by 7 am. Factor in getting gas, snack breaks, and piss breaks. They should be in Vegas at 1 PM. If they stop to pick up the "supplies" for, say, 30 minutes, they could be back in Pine Hollow by 8 PM. Collect

Eli's scoot and be done with everything before 10 PM. That worked for him.

"Okay, we can work with that," he replied to Dan, "What about money? Do we have to pay for this pickup?"

"Nah, Nah, all taken care of; I use a crypto app to pay. No need for you guys to be carrying any of my money."

'Fine suits me," said Rex. The last thing he needed was the responsibility of traveling with the cash. What if it got lost or stolen? Could he trust this Cody? How reliable was he?

'Any questions?" asked Dan

Rex looked at Clay. Clay shook his head, "Nah, I think we are good," Rex replied, "I guess we will let you guys get on with whatever you do here. We will back around, say 630am?"

Dan looked at Cody, "6.30 work for you, Cody?"

"Yeah, see you then," Cody said, "Don't be late."

Rex and Cody said their goodbyes and decided to hit the Dead Crow saloon for a beer before turning in and getting an early night. The hippy kid was there, no sign of Nina.

They decided to order some Nachos while they drank their beers.

"What do you make of this Vegas run?" Clay asked Rex as they munched on their nachos.

"Dunno, I assume they are legit. If they wanted to kill us, they could have done it the other night. Perhaps reliable guys are hard to come by in this town?" said Rex.

"Yeah, I think you're probably right," Clay replied, washing down his food with another swig of beer.

CHAPTER 18

5.30 am came way too soon. Rex groaned as he got up to shut off the alarm app on his cell phone. Fuck he needed some coffee. The motel room provided a little one-man coffee pot and a packet of what was passed for coffee. Rex already knew it would probably suck, but he was willing to risk it anyways.

He took a piss and brushed his teeth while waiting for the little coffee maker to work its magic. Meanwhile, somehow, Clay managed to sleep through all the noise. Rex wasn't sure how he did it. If the shoe was on the other foot, he would have been wide awake the moment his alarm had gone off.

Rex pulled on his jeans, then his biker boots. He grabbed the freshly made coffee in its disposal cup and took a sip, which, surprisingly, was, was not bad. He left the motel and took a quick review of his bike. Nothing had shaken loose since he last rode it. Everything seemed as it should be. He checked his cell phone for the route to Vegas. He and the rest of the Tucson chapter had done the run to Vegas multiple times, except he had never done it from Pine Hollow – always via Phoenix and Wickenburg – this was a first for him.

As far as he could tell, they would take the 77 over to Highway 40, bringing them past Flagstaff, and then they would join Highway 93, which was the road Rex was familiar with. He tried to think back about traffic stops and where the local law enforcement liked to hide out and made a mental note of those spots. Rex turned and went back into the Motel room, only to find Clay up and pretty much ready to roll.

"Checking your scoot?" asked Clay

"Yeah, think we are good to go. Are you about ready?" Rex asked his club brother.

Clay left his helmet in their room. Rex did a quick look over the room to make sure he wasn't forgetting anything.

"Got your cell phone?" he asked Clay.

"Yeah, right here," Clay replied, tapping his jeans pocket.

"Alright, let's go, nuts to butts all the way to Dan's warehouse."

The ride took them all over 3 minutes; no traffic at this hour of the morning, Rex noted.

To their surprise, Cody was already at the warehouse when they arrived just after 6 am. Parked out front was a small florist van; Rex assumed that's what they would be traveling in.

"Morning, boys," Cody greeted them 'All set for this?"

"I think so," Rex replied, "I've mapped the quickest way there; just keep in mind I will have to stop every 100 or so miles to refuel."

Cody looked at Rex's motorcycle as if he could calculate fuel usage from staring at it. 'Okay," was all he said.

"You wanna give me the address in Vegas?" asked Rex

"Yeah, that would help," chuckled Cody; he handed Rex a crumpled piece of paper from his back pocket. Rex punched the address into his GPS, noticing it was in a town called Summerlin and not central Vegas.

"You got a headset for that thing," asked Cody, nodding at Rex's cell phone.

"Actually, I don't," Rex replied

"Hold on then," said Cody, going back into the warehouse. He returned a few minutes later with a used headset and earpiece combo.

"Wanna try it before we leave?" he asked.

Rex plugged it into his cell phone. Put the earpiece in his right ear and pulled on his helmet. He then speed-dialed Clay. Clay's phone rang seconds later. "Hello, hello," Rex said, just making sure he could hear Clay speak before hanging up.

"Yeah, it seems to work okay," Rex replied.

"Very good," said Cody, "So I say ride up ahead of us, say half a mile or so and call in immediately if you see anything at all suspicious."

'Yeah, will do," Rex replied.

"I will be driving just over the speed limit, no more than, say, 5 miles faster at any given time," Cody explained.

"Won't that attract the cop's attention?" asked Clay

"Eh, I doubt it. We find if you drive EXACTLY on the speed limit, that can be as bad as speeding. Unless you are a little old lady, no one meets the speed limit," Cody replied.

"Want me to check if your brake lights work before we leave?" asked Rex, "Seems to me traffic cops always pull you over for faulty brake lights or a loose license plate,"

"Good thinking, buddy, but I checked this morning before leaving the house; thanks," said Cody, "You boys ready to do this?"

'Yeah' let's hit the road," Rex replied.

As they pulled away from the warehouse, Main Street was starting to come alive. Shopkeepers and store owners are going about their morning routines. Soon, they were on Highway 40, heading west. Rex marveled at how beautiful this part of Arizona was: luscious green grass and tall pine trees. Nothing like the landscape of his native Tucson; it was almost like they were in a different state.

Every 30 minutes, he called in with Clay, who was riding a shotgun while Cody drove the little florist van.

At Flagstaff, they stopped to refuel and grab breakfast. The two bikers made small talk with Cody as they ate. It turns out Cody was born and raised in Pine Hollow and went to school with Dan Thatcher, who had been a bully even in high school. No surprise there. Rex had never liked bullies, and this made him despise Dan even more.

They finished breakfast, and Clay paid. Once more, before setting off, he reminded Rex to call in if he noticed anything out of place on the roads. He also reminded them both that he would be riding 5 miles per hour faster than the suggested speed limit. Rex told him he had not forgotten the instructions and fired up his scoot for the next leg of the journey.

Rex rode along with no music playing on his phone. He always preferred to just tune in to the sound his engine made as he rode; that was true music to his ears. He soaked up the views as he kept an eye open for cops or "anything out of the norm," but so far, so good.

Once they made it to Highway 93, Rex noticed traffic cops parked between the North and South lanes, but they were facing the Southbound lanes. Regardless, he hit speed dial on his gas tank-mounted phone and gave Clay the heads up. He could hear Clay advising Cody as they drove. He then hung up his phone and continued driving.

They passed a sign for a well-known tourist attraction, "Fire a 50 caliber rifle," and perhaps next time he and Clay were in this neck of the woods, they would go for that. Looked like a fun day out. He also noticed that they offered a tank you could drive. He definitely wanted to do that, too.

Shortly after the 50-caliber ranch, they had to stop again for him to refuel. He needed a break to stretch his legs and loosen his back up, which was starting to feel tight. He notified Clay which gas station they were pulling into, and moments later, he saw their little florist van pull into the car park.

"GPS says less than an hour to go," Rex explained, "Let's take 5," Clay nodded his approval of the idea, but Cody looked less than impressed. Rex thought about it for a moment, and Clay was probably more restless than the rest of them sometimes; just sitting here doing nothing was more boring than riding or driving.

'Male it quick," advised Cody.

After gassing up, Rex hit the restroom, took a piss and grabbed a soda from the fridge to guzzle before they hit the road again. It was alright for Cody and Clay as they had AC in their little van where Rex was exposed to the elements on his Harley. He was glad it was not summertime.

The last hour of their ride to the stash house was uneventful. Rex always liked this part of the journey. Rolling landscapes with magnificent mountains off in the distance. Then, one big turn and you will start to see the suburbs of Las Vegas. Rex speed-dialed Clay to tell him traffic was starting to pick up, making it a lot harder to spot Law enforcement, especially if you factor in under-covers and plain-clothes cops. His last words to Clay were 'Stay frosty."

He pulled off the exit ramp and followed the GPS through the ever-growing suburbs of Vegas. Even since the last time he visited Sin City, he felt like the place had tripled in size. He guessed that much like Arizona, Californians fleeing their state's disastrous political policies were taking advantage of the tax breaks afforded to them in Nevada, which had caused the vast majority of the rapid influx of new people to Vegas. Finally, he came to a nondescript suburban house. He double-checked the GPS to make sure it was in the right spot. Instead of immediately stopping, he phoned Clay to let them know he had arrived. Then he casually cruised up the street and back, looking into each car parked on the street to make sure no one was monitoring them. Seemed all clear, so he circled back. As he did so, he saw Cody and Clay pulling up from their florist's van.

Cody got out, and when he saw Rex about to dismount his bike, he held up his hand in the "Stop" gesture and instructed him 'Wait here." Rex nodded that he understood.

Cody buzzed on the resident's front door. From the angle he was on, Rex couldn't see who answered, but he stayed vigilant. Ever since he was a teen and watched Scarface, he was understandably wary of large-scale drug purchases. Cody returned empty-handed.

'We gotta circle round back," he explained to Rex, "Follow me."

Rex waited until Cody was back in the van and kicked his scoot into gear. He slowly rolled after them as they went up the street. He made a quick left turn, followed by another down a back alley that ran parallel to the suburban homes. He saw Cody slow down at the back gate of one of the places and come to a stop himself.

He pondered posting up outside, but in the end, he decided to ride into the backyard, following Cody and Clay. The moment he rolled into the yard, some white trash kid he hadn't noticed earlier appeared and dragged the gate shut behind him. He kept one eye out for men with chainsaws. *Again, I wish he had packed his Glock for this trip.* He felt naked without it.

Two more guys appeared from the back door of the place. Rex couldn't hear what they said to Cody, but judging from their body language, everything seemed kosher.

They must have asked Cody about him and Clay, as he could see Cody explaining that they were there for him. He shut down his bike, pulled off his helmet and went to introduce himself.

"Hey, I'm Rex," he said, holding out his hand. The two newcomers just stared at him and nodded. *Fine, I guess I'll go fuck myself, then* thought Rex. Despite being a one percenter, he hated rudeness. You make the effort to be nice to someone, and they throw that back on your face? Fuck them.

The two men dipped back inside with Cody. Rex looked over to Clay, who was staying put in the van and just shrugged. Rex assumed they were not keen on letting newcomers know about the layout of their house for security reasons.

Moments later, Cody returned carrying two of those medium-sized U-haul boxes.

"Need any help?" Rex asked

Cody quickly shook his head. The two other men came out from the back door as well, carrying similar U-haul boxes.

Cody returned to the house and came out moments later with 2 more U-haul boxes. *This is ridiculous. I thought Rex and I could be there, speeding up the process.* Just as he finished thinking that, Cody shut the rear doors of the van and said his goodbyes to the other guys. Mister Tweaker on the rear gate dragged it open once again and gestured for them to back up. Rex rolled out of the way, put his helmet back on and followed Clay and Cody out of the backyard. The gate behind him clanged shut as soon as his rear wheel entered the alleyway.

That's it? Thought Rex – *that little van could at least hold 5 times as many U-haul boxes as they managed to pack inside it. Why so few?* He would ask Cody when they stopped next.

Traffic coming out of Las Vegas started to thicken up as rush hour started. Rex didn't want to take any chances of them getting into a fender bender was a commuter too busy messing with their cell phone than concentrating on driving. He was sure it was a daily occurrence on the roads, and the last thing he wanted was for Cody and Clay to be involved in one. He just wanted to get the shipment back to Pine Hollow and get Samantha's chopper off Dan, and be done with these yokels.

Halfway home, they stopped at a truck service that had an adjoining Subway sandwich store. Cody offered to buy them an early dinner, which Rex was grateful for since he hadn't eaten in about 12 hours.

"So what's up with the size of the shiPMents?' asked Rex, "I thought we would be bringing way more back with us."

"Oh, Dan likes to get a product in and move it fast," Cody explained, "No sense in sitting on a bunch and getting raided, eh?"

"Yeah, true, I guess," Rex replied, thinking. *Heck, even with this much, we are all looking at lengthy prison sentences; much more wasn't going to make a difference if we got caught.*

"He knows just how much each town on Highway 77 needs," Cody explains, "But if we get caught short, we can make a quick trip back out to Vegas."

"I get ya," said Clay, "It's like supermarkets these days; supposedly, they only keep a 3-day supply of anything. That's why if there is ever a storm or a disaster, they run out."

'Yeah, kinda like that," Cody replied between mouthfuls of his foot-long sandwich.

"So, how long have you been doing these runs for Dan?" asked Rex

"Oh, for a while, I guess," said Cody, "Beats working a regular job, ya know?"

"Yeah, I get it," Rex replied, finishing off his soda and being grateful to take a break from riding.

Cody looked over their trays of food. "You boys nearly ready to hit the road? Starting to get dark now."

Rex looked over at Clay, who nodded, "Yeah, let's do it."

The ride home through the mountains back to Pine Hollow was uneventful. By the time they were pulling into the loading dock of Dan's warehouse, Rex's butt and back were starting to hurt. It had been a long day. They had done it, and now it was time to get things sorted with Dan.

As Rex pulled off his helmet, Cody and Clay got out of the van.

"Hey, give us a hand, would ya?" Cody asked of Rex.

'Sure, give me a sec," he replied, placing his helmet on his handlebars. It felt good to walk around again and get the blood circulating in his legs.

In two trips, the van was unloaded, and the boxes were sitting in the office next door to Dan's.

Rex and Clay stood and watched as Dan opened the U-Haul boxes and inspected their contents. Rex noted a lot of bottles of prescription pills were in this delivery. He recalled reading an article where young kids today wouldn't smoke pot or snort coke but would happily pop Oxys and Vicodin. Youth of today, eh?

After Dan was happy with the shiPMent, Rex asked if he could have a quick word with him in private. Dan agreed and led Rex into his office next door.

"So what's up, bro?" Dan asked Rex after they had both taken seats on either side of Dan's desk.

"So we did what was asked of us. We are all squared off now, eh?" said Rex.

"What? Uh, not really. This isn't a one-and-done thing, brother." Dan replied, "Think of this as a partial down payment."

"You said you needed us to do security work, and we did it," Rex replied, flabbergasted that Dan would move the goalposts on him.

"Hey, hey, calm down. I'm sorry if I didn't make it clear to you, but I need you to do more than just one run, sheesh," said Dan.

Rex tried to retain his composure, "So what are we talking about here? We need to be back in Tucson at some point."

Dan thought for a moment, "Hm, fair enough. I tell you what. Do 3 more runs for me, and we will call it even, cool?"

"So, to be clear, we go to Vegas with Cody 3 more times, and you will consider that payment in full for that $3000 dollar bike out there?" asked Rex wanting to make sure there was no more bullshit.

"Yes, sir. You have my word on it," Dan replied, extending his hand for Rex to shake.

"So we are here 3 more weeks then?" asked Rex wanting to clarify before shaking this fuckers hand.

"Nah, Nah, nothing like that. Let's say 2 runs next week and 1 the week after, and we are good, okay? Dan replied.

"Ok, fair enough. Done deal," said Rex, shaking Dan's hand.

Rex got up and left Dan's office, and he nodded to Clay that they were all done and walked out of the building. Clay followed behind him.

"Dude, dude, what about the bike?" he asked

"Keep walking," Rex hissed to Clay as he headed for his scoot.

Rex gave Clay a ride back to their motel. Only once they had arrived did he bother to explain to Clay

"Yeah, so fuck face back there wants us to do 3 more runs before he gives us Eli's chopper," Rex explained.

Clay whistled, "3 more? So what? We are stuck here for another month?"

"Nah. Dan says no more than 10 days," Rex explained, "2 runs next week and 1 more the week after."

"Oh, that's kinda doable. What about your job?" Clay asked.

"I'll call in the morning and explain to my boss. He's gonna be pissed, but then again, I'll be losing money by staying out so long, so I'm gonna be pissed too," said Rex.

Clay checked his phone for the time, "Shit, man, let's hit the bar and grab some food before it's too late."

"Yeah, good call," Rex replied. He quickly entered their motel room and tossed his helmet and riding gloves on the bed before locking the door and following Clay down Main Street to the Dead Crow Saloon.

CHAPTER 19

Friday was a write-off. The pair got up early to get breakfast. Rex was surprised at how sore his body was after 12 hours of riding. They hit their diner for the $3.50 breakfast, came back to their motel room and just watched TV in between napping. At 6 PM, they finally left the motel in search of food before all of their options closed for the weekend. They found a little hole-in-the-wall spot that served them home-cooked spaghetti and meatballs. A welcome change from Burgers and Gas Station food options.

After that, they hit the Dead Crow, which was actually pretty packed. So there were people in this small town. Rex scanned the room for talent but didn't see any ladies that caught his eye. Oh well. He wasn't there to get laid. They ended up sitting by the bar chatting with Nina for most of the night. They staggered home just before closing time.

Saturday morning, Rex was hungover. He went and sat in the motel's hot tub to try and sweat out all the toxins in his body. No clue as to whether there was any science to it or not, but he actually felt a lot better afterward.

Clay, the lazy bastard, finally was waking up when Rex returned to the room. Of course, he was starving, so they did their daily ritual of walking to their diner. Apparently, they had missed breakfast and had to choose something from the lunch menu. Clay went with the meatloaf, and Rex ordered a roast beef sandwich, which was surprisingly decent.

After returning to the motel, Clay announced that he was going to take a nap. Rex decided it would be a good time to work on his bike; he wanted it to be in top shape for their next Vegas run. He grabbed his tool roll and went back out to the car park.

Rex was so engrossed in tuning his engine that he didn't hear the car pull up near him nor the footfalls of the man approaching. He did, however, hear the voice that asked him.

"Can I help you?"

Rex looked up; it was a local sheriff. "I dunno, know anything about Harleys?" he asked the Sheriff.

"Listen, wise-ass," raged the local cop, "I asked you what you are doing here."

"Well, right now, I am working on my bike, and other than that, I am just visiting your little town," Rex explained. As a one percenter, he was used to unnecessary harassment from Law Enforcement individuals.

"Oh yeah, where are you visiting from?" the cop demanded to know.

I'm from down south," Rex replied nonchalantly.

"Funny, you don't look Mexican," snipped the Sheriff.

"Down south but North of the Border, Mister Sheriff," said Rex, standing up and extending a greasy hand for the man to shake.

The Sheriff looked at his hand in disgust, "Listen, scum bag, we don't take kindly to troublemakers in this town, so just watch your step."

"I'll keep that in mind," said Rex. He noticed the man's name tag said "Thatcher" on it.

"Hey, any relation to Dan?" Clay asked the Sheriff, who nodded at his name tag.

"Dan? What? You know Dan? He's my little brother," the man replied.

"No way! Small world, eh?" Rex smiled, trying to deescalate the situation, "Me and my buddy are doing some work for him,"

"No shit, very cool," said the Sheriff, finally starting to loosen up. "Nice to meet ya. My name is Calvin," He extended his hand for Rex to shake.

Rex grabbed a microfiber cleaning cloth from his tool roll and gave his right hand a wipe down. He shook Calvin's hand.

"Nice to meet ya, Sheriff. And don't worry. We tend to keep the peace way more than disturb the peace," Rex tried to do his best earnest smile to put the law enforcement officer at ease.

"Good to know," smiled Calvin, the Sheriff.

Calvin stood over Rex for a minute longer than was comfortable before finally wandering off back to his cop car. Rex kept one eye on the man as he pretended to work on his bike until the cop car left the car park. *Fuck that, Guy* Rex swore under his breath. He had dealt with all sorts of cops over the years: Mean, kind, sensible, vicious and super smart. This cop was as dirty as they come. He and Clay would have to keep their wits about them until they left this town.

That afternoon, while chilling on his motel bed watching TV with Clay, Rex heard his cell phone go. He grabbed his phone and checked it. Sure enough, a text from Dan Thatcher. "Monday morning, 7 am."

Rex knew immediately what it meant. Another run to Las Vegas. He just wanted to get these commitments to the Rednecks done, get Eli's chopper back. Fulfill his promise to his dead friend. He gave it to his daughter and went home. He texted the crime boss back right away, "Sure thing. 7 am Monday." If Dan lived up to his word, then after this, there would be two more runs, and then he would be done. One later in the week and one the following week. Definitely do-able.

That evening, they ate dinner in a local diner and then headed to the Dead Crow Saloon for a few beers. Nina, Hippy Kid and some large cowboy were behind the bar slinging drinks. There were no seats by the bar, so Rex grabbed them a booth, and Clay went up and ordered them some beers and whiskey shots.

After a few drinks, Rex felt fine.

"Hey, remember that time we were about 18 and went to that party at the Catalina Foothills?" Rex asked Clay

"Oh, at that super-rich chick's house?" Clay replied.

"That's the one!" said Rex, "How old were we? 18? 19?"

"Yeah, something like that," laughed Clay, "That was a great party,"

"Yeah, we had just started hanging around with the Steel Reapers, and most of our friends were terrified of us," laughed Rex

"Yeah, the guys at that party all hated us. All their girlfriends wanted Harley rides, and we were happy to oblige!" added Clay

I think we got chased out of the foothills that night, right?" asked Rex.

"Ha ha, we did too. That said, pretty much half the parties we attended in our Senior year ended in fights or getting chased out with baseball bats," said Clay.

"How the fuck are we still alive after that?" laughed Rex

"Haha, someone up there is looking out for us, I guess," said Clay, downing another shot of Whiskey.

It was true; they had survived some crazy nights that would have had a lesser man. *Luck of the Irish or something,* thought Rex as he sipped on his beer.

At 10 PM, Nina came over with a tray of beers and more shots, "On me, boys," she said as she slid into their booth next to Clay.

"Thanks, Nina," said Clay, grabbing the beers and passing them out to everyone. He then did the same with the shot glasses and held his high. "Cheers," he said, toasting both Nina and Rex.

They both followed his lead, raising their shot glasses and toasting Clay back.

"Hey, what are you guys doing Sunday afternoon?' asked Nina

"Why? You asking us out on a double date?' asked Rex cheekily.

"Him, maybe not you," Nina replied, winking at Rex. "No, I was thinking you guys could meet Samantha. You know, that's the reason why you are here and all that."

"Hmm, that would be cool. I'm down," Clay replied, "What about you, Rex?"

Rex thought for a moment. They haven't had Eli's chopper back from Dan Thatcher yet. He wanted to give her that bike when he first met her. Well, that bike would be hers in another 10 days. *What harm would it bring to meet her now?* They could just not tell her they were meant to be giving her a motorcycle from her dead father.

"Sure, we could do that," Rex replied, "What restaurant were you thinking?"

"Oh, I thought you guys could come to the house, and perhaps we could go for a picnic. There are some gorgeous national parks and forests around here," explained Nina.

"We don't have any food back in our motel room. Would the supermarkets even be open tomorrow," asked Rex.

"Don't worry, just bring yourselves. I'll take care of the rest," Nina reassured the pair.

"Okay, as long as you are okay with it, then sure!' Rex replied. Chinking his beer glass on Nina's.

"Hey, I gotta get back to work. Break time is over. Give me your cell phone, Clay," said Nina

Clay fished his cell phone out of his jeans pocket and handed it to Nina. She punched in her phone number. Perhaps she actually liked Clay, after all? Thought Rex to himself.

"Okay, text me tomorrow around lunchtime, and I'll give you directions to our place. It's walking distance, so you won't need to ride," she reassured the two bikers before sliding out from the booth and returning to the bar.

"See you tomorrow," Rex said as they watched her leave them.

CHAPTER 20

Sunday, Rex woke with a massive hangover. In fact, he felt like dog shit.

"I can't keep doing this to myself," he said out loud.

Clay groaned in the bed across the room from him, "Ughhh, kill me. Kill me now."

"What? You too?' asked Rex. He couldn't remember the last time Clay was hungover.

"I'm dying, bro, dying, I tell you," groaned Clay from under the covers.

Rex jumped up out of bed and grabbed two of the disposable paper coffee cups the motel provided. He went to the bathroom and filled them both with tap water. He downed his and refilled it. Taking them both back into the main room, he went to Clay's bed and handed him one. "Here, drink this," he said. Rex also made a mental note to go buy some bottles of water for the room so they wouldn't need to drink nasty ass tap water again.

'Dude, get up and put on your shorts; we need to hit the hot tub," Rex said to Clay.

"Ughh, don't think I can move, man," Clay groaned.

"No, trust me. You'll feel better afterward," Rex demanded.

After 5 minutes of begging for Clay to get his ass out of bed and outside, he finally relented. Rex made them both cups of instant coffee in their little coffee maker and took them outside with them. After 30 minutes of sitting out in the morning sun, the hot tub blasting all the toxins out of their poor, abused bodies, Clay announced he was actually feeling better.

'Fuck me, you were right," Clay exclaimed, "I can feel the poison leaving my body."

"See, I told ya," said Rex, who was relieved he was starting to feel better, too.

"How did you figure this out?" Clay asked.

"I dunno, man, just happened, I guess," Rex replied. "You know, I used to know this guy who was a chef."

"Uh, okay," said Clay

"He told me once, alcohol is a poison," Rex continued, "I was like. A poison? Are you kidding me? Alcohol is delicious."

"You got that right," said Clay

'Yeah, but the more I know now, the more I think maybe he was on to something," explained Rex.

"Well, if you told me this morning, I would have definitely agreed with ya," said Clay

"So, what's up with you and Nina?' asked Rex.

"Me and Nina? What? Nothing! Well, at least as far as I am aware," said Clay 'Why, why do you ask?"

"Ah, cuz I just think she is into you," Rex explained.

"Really? I must have missed the signs," said Clay.

'Story of your life," Rex replied.

Rex looked at the position of the sun in the sky. It had to be nearly lunchtime. "Hey, we should get out and start getting ready," he suggested.

"Yeah, good thinking," Clay replied, "I should text Nina too and get her address,"

"Sounds like a plan," Rex replied.

"So what do you think of meeting Eli's daughter?" asked Clay, still sitting in the hot tub.

"Eh, can't hurt, man." Rex replied, "We just don't tell her about Eli's bike, ya know?"

"But we're gonna give it to her!' Clay replied.

"Yes, dumbass, but think about it." Rex replied, "We don't actually have it yet. What if there are problems? We can't tell her about the bike until we have it. You get me?"

"So you think we might have problems with Dan and his boys?' asked Clay

"Well, I hope not," said Rex, "But until we actually get the bike back, we shouldn't be getting her hopes up."

"Okay, so no mention of it," Clay reiterated.

'Yes, correct," said Rex, "Look, Dan is a criminal. He has no idea what that bike is worth. That said, he did shake on it, and a man's word is his bond. We have to operate on the understanding he will keep his word."

"I get ya," Clay replied.

"However, if he doesn't, well....that's when the trouble will start for him and his cronies," said Rex.

"Steel Reaper trouble," Clay added.

"You know what I'm talking about," Rex replied, nodding at Clay, "C'mon, let's get out of this hot tub and go meet Eli's daughter, Samantha."

"I'm ready; I am actually starting to wrinkle like a prune," said Clay, stepping out of the hot tub and grabbing a towel.

"Yeah, let's go, prune boy," said Rex 'There's no point us grabbing breakfast now; we will be eating with Nina and Samantha soon enough," toweling himself off too.

"Okay, let's head back to our room, and I'll text her," said Clay, dripping water as he walked back to the room.

CHAPTER 21

Sure enough, Nina's house was, in fact, within walking distance of their motel. Clay and Rex had followed her instructions, and it wasn't far off the main street. Rex vaguely recalled Nina pointing out her street when they walked her back home from the bar the first night they had met her.

Rex let Clay ring the buzzer on the front door of her small but tidy house.

Nina answered the door, looking well-rested and dressed smartly. It was like she was wearing different makeup from her usual "Dive Bar Biker rock n roll" gear.

'Wow, you look nice," Clay complimented her; she smiled.

"Yeah, you scrub up pretty well," added Rex.

'Aww, thanks, 'Nina replied, "You boys look well rested. I honestly thought you might not make it today. You were both pretty toasty last night."

"Oh, believe me, we were rouuughhhh this morning," Rex smiled, "Nothing a good session in the hot tub couldn't cure."

'Oh, you have a hot tub? I wish I had known!" Nina replied 'They're the best."

Rex looked around Nina's living room. Simple but nicely decorated.

"Hey, not bad," he stated

"Thanks, you're not bad yourself," she teased.

"I mean the room, not you smarty pants," Rex deadpanned

'Aww, spoilsport," Nina pouted.

"Well, I think you look great, screw what Rex has to say," Clay interjected.

"Nice save, bud," Nina replied.

'So, how long ya lived here?" Rex asked the sassy barmaid.

"Hmm, 25 years or so," Nina replied

'Whoa, no shit," Clay replied.

" I was actually born in Milwaukee," Nina started, "My dad was a doctor, and Mom was a stay-at-home mom raising 4 daughters."

"That's cool," so Rex, "So how did ya end up in Arizona?'

"Well," Nina said, "Even though my dad was a highly respected doctor, the stress of being in the Emergency room 24-7 got to him. He started drinking a lot and coming home, taking it out on my mom."

"Oh shit, sorry to hear that," Rex replied. He hated bullies and men who couldn't hold their liquor.

"So eventually, mom got tired of the beatings and abuse. She packed us all up in her car, and we drove out west, ending up in Flagstaff."

"That's a nice town," said Clay

"Yeah, definitely," Nina added, "Unfortunately, trying to raise 4 kids on a basic wage was super tough for my mom. So the moment we could, all of us kids had to get jobs and help out. I ended up waitressing at 16 and becoming a barmaid at 18."

"No shit," said Clay

Yeah, then I met a guy, and he convinced me to move to Phoenix with him. There's more money in bartending in Phoenix, was his logic," Nina explained.

Rex thought about it for a moment, "Well, he was probably right."

"Yeah, he was. But then he ended up banging my best friend," said Nina.

"Oh wow, one of them," said Rex.

"Yep, one of them," said Nina, "I moved out, and that's when I met Samantha's mother, Lora, and we became best friends."

'I was wondering about that," said Rex.

"So then, a few years after Samantha was born, we decided to move up here for a more quiet life," Nina explained.

"'That's cool; I can see the appeal," said Rex. "Better quality of life raising a kid outside of the big cities."

'That's what Lora was thinking!" Nina replied, "My mother was getting older, so I moved up to be closer to her."

'That makes sense," said Clay, nodding his head in approval.

"Oh Geez, look at the time," said Nina. "You boys must be starving; I had better grab Samantha and get ready."

"Ok, cool, thanks," said Clay. "Yeah, now that I think about it, I am kinda starving."

Nina disappeared into the back of the house. He could hear her pounding on a door in the back of the house, either waking Samantha or getting her off her cell phone.

He looked over to Clay and shrugged. Meeting the orphan daughter of your former mentor and club wasn't something he did on a regular basis, and he was currently feeling pretty damn uncomfortable. Would she hold him responsible for Eli's death? Would she blame him and Clay, well, the club, for keeping him away from his fatherly responsibilities? Issues like this played on him.

Nina reappeared with a sulky, sullen teenager, Samantha.

"Everyone, this is Samantha. Samantha, these men were your dad's friends from Tucson, Rex and Clay," she said, pointing to Rex on the couch and Clay sitting on the chair next to the couch.

"Hi, Samantha," said Rex and Clay in unison

"You can call me Sam," Samantha replied.

"Okay, Sam," said Rex. 'Supposedly, Nina is taking us on a picnic."

"Yeah, I heard, whatever," Samantha replied.

'Speaking of, Let me get everything ready. Sam, stay and talk to the boys while I get everything prepped," said Nina, excusing herself and retreating to the kitchen.

"So, what do you do?" asked Rex

'What do you mean what do I do?" she asked.

"Oh, like, do you work, go to school, that type of thing?" Rex explained.

"Well, I graduate High School this Summer," said Samantha. "Oh, I also work part-time at the local supermarket.

"Wow, multi-talented," said Rex, trying to get her to loosen up.

"Yeah, well, I want to go to art school in Phoenix this fall," explained Samantha, "and that takes money."

"It sure does," said Rex, "You have been to Phoenix before?"

"Yeah, Mom, ah, Nina took me down there to see this band Slipknot," she explained, "So much more to do in Phoenix than here."

'Slipknot, cool," Clay commented.

"Do you even know what they sound like?" she asked

"Of course," smiled Clay, " me and Rex actually did some security work for them when they played Tucson a few times."

"No way! You met the band?" she asked all of a sudden, interested in what they had to say.

"Yeah, we used to do part-time work at the local arena back home, running security teams for metal bands. We have met Korn, Slayer, and a few others," Rex said.

'Slipknot was the best, though, right?" asked Samantha.

"The singer was cool, little guy," said Rex

"Cory Taylor!' exclaimed Samantha.

"The only one I didn't like was that drummer who died," said Clay, "He was a little prick."

"Joey Jorgenson! Oh my god, you met Joey??" asked Samantha.

"Yeah, never like that guy. He would literally piss his pants backstage all the time. The arena cleaning crew hated him."

"Wow, I can't believe you met Cory and Joey," Samantha blurted. "What about Clown? Did you meet Clown?"

"No idea who that one was," said Clay. "I mean, I saw him with the mask on but not without."

"Wow, you guys are so cool," said Samantha.

Nina came out of the kitchen with 2 coolers that looked pretty heavy.

"Hey, one of you guys wanna give me a hand?" she asked.

Clay jumped up and took both coolers from her.

'I got ya," he said. "Lead the way."

Nina led Clay out the front of her house and down the side to where her beat-up Jeep was parked.

"Here, throw them in the back," she instructed Clay. "Thanks for helping."

"No problem: Clay replied.

'Wait here, let me go grab Sam and Rex," she said, heading back to the house.

Sam and Rex followed Nina back out to the car, and Clay took the seat next to Nina up front, leaving Rex and Sam to take the back seats. She took them down Main Street, heading North, and turned right on one of the side streets before Main Street ran out. The road she took was a long and winding one deep into the pines. Once again, Rex had to admire the beauty of Northern Arizona. So different from what he was used to.

After about 20 minutes of driving, she pulled off the main road and took a dirt road between the pines. Rex assumed it was one of those fire break trails foresters created in the advent of a forest fire. It was certainly not something that any tourist passing through town would ever stumble upon.

Nina soon found the spot she was looking for, and her run-down jeep came to a halt.

"Alright, we are here," she announced, "This is my favorite spot to get away and clear my head. No people, no noise, no nothing."

"I am digging it," said Clay. "We have nothing like this back in Tucson."

"Tucson is cool," said Nina, "Great food down there."

"Yeah, we have some of the best Mexican food in the southwest," Clay replied.

Rex helped Samantha take the picnic supplies out from the back of the Jeep. He had been on many camping trips with the club, but he couldn't recall the last time he had a picnic. Age 9? Age 10? Years and years ago, basically.

Nina laid out a blanket for them. Clay looked around, admiring the clearing between the pines and the mountain views.

"Say, any bears around here?" he asked somewhat nervously.

"I've never seen any bears, but definitely some bobcats," said Nina. "I've heard wolves too, but usually after sunset. Never see 'em, though. Probably more scared of us than we are of them."

"You got a piece on you?" asked Clay, looking around nervously.

"I do, but I left it at home. I thought you big tough bikers were not scared of anyone or anything," Nina teased.

"Ha ha very funny," said Clay, still not convinced.

Lunch was good. Nina made some great sandwiches, such as turkey, Swiss cheese, tomato, lettuce, and pickles, on some freshly baked bread, with homemade mac and cheese and potato salad. Rex and Clay hadn't eaten this well in weeks. They washed it all down with beers from Nina's cooler as Samantha sipped on a soda.

After eating, Nina proclaimed, "Oof, I need to walk all this food off. Clay, come with me."

"But I wanna chill here," he moaned.

"Don't be a big baby," she teased. "Get up; it will do you some good."

"Besides," added Rex, "Walking will help your digestion. Go on, get going."

After Clay and Nina walked off into the pines, Samantha turned to Rex.

"So you guys grew up with my dad?" she asked.

"Yeah, he was the best. A huge influence on Clay and me," Rex replied.

"Really?" She asked. Samantha seemed surprised by this.

'Yeah, did you get to spend much time with him?" he asked.

"Eh, not really. I have a few vague memories from being super young, but that's about it." Samantha replied.

"Oh, sorry to hear it," said Rex. He figured it had to be tough not to grow up with a dad. Especially someone so legendary as Eli.

"Ehhh, it was cool. Mom had "Uncle" Steve, and then after Mom passed, I had Nina. She had her problems with pills and whatnot, but she tried her best."

"Ah, I see," said Rex, trying to be understanding.

'What did your mom tell you about your biological father?' Rex asked curiously.

"Hmm, that he was a biker. He was in the Steel Reapers Motorcycle Club. After the cops beat him down in Phoenix, he was warned to never come back. That he made motorcycles," She listed off pretty much everything she could remember about Eli.

Rex remembered being beaten down by the Phoenix cops. While he wasn't there, he had heard most of the story. Eli had stood up to a bully with a badge, and when the lone cop couldn't take Eli down, his cop buddies jumped in and used their billy clubs. He was in hospital for a week recovering from his injuries, and after that, he was always wary about passing through the Phoenix Metro area.

"He was tough as nails, your father," Rex told Samantha.

"Yeah, that's what I heard," said Samantha.

'So, what do you want to do at Art school?" Rex asked Samantha.

"I dunno, I just like art, I guess. My favorite subject at school. Maybe pin striping on hot rods? Maybe customize motorcycle helmets? Maybe Motorcycle gas tanks?" Samantha replied.

'Wow, you really are your father's daughter!" Rex replied, laughing. Funny that normally, the apple doesn't fall far from the tree.

Finally, Nina and Clay reappeared from their "walk."

"Hey, we should think about packing it up soon," suggested Nina, "It will be getting dark in a bit."

"Sounds good to me," said Rex, getting up and throwing their empty beer cans into a trash bag Nina had provided.

As they drove back, Rex commented to Nina, "Hey, you have lived here for so long. You know, the place like a local."

'Ehh, not really. Small towns like this are funny," she explained, keeping her eyes on the fire break trail between the pines in the now dimming light.

'Some people grow up in places like Pine Hollow and can't wait to leave and never come back. Others leave and travel the world only to realize what they had at home was the best after all. Some never leave and look their noses down on anyone from out of town. Even if they have lived here for 20-something years," she explained.

"I assume you mean the Thatcher brothers?" asked Rex.

"You assumed right," Nina laughed.

"Oh boy, have they always been that bad?" asked Rex

"My friends who went to school with them have told me yes. They have always been a nightmare for this town," Nina replied. "Like if there's a god or something, why can't god just strike them down?"

"Yeah, I hear ya; there's a lot of people out there I would like to see get hit by a random bolt of lightning or something," said Rex.

"Sometimes I feel there is no justice in this world," Nina added.

"Ehhh. Feels that way sometimes," Rex replied, "But I have seen karma knock down someone who deserves it time and time again. I feel like it always works out. In the end."

Nina dropped Rex and Clay at their motel, and they thanked both Nina and Samantha for a fun day out. They are not their normal Sunday afternoon activities, but sometimes, to do something new is good for the soul.

'We should get some sleep soon," Rex said to Clay. "Another run first thing tomorrow morning."

"Sounds good to me," Clay replied. "I'm beaten."

CHAPTER 22

Rex woke up at 6 am and did a prison-style workout in the car park before waking up Rex. Burpees and push-ups were great exercises when you didn't have access to a gym and needed to get a workout in. Rex knew he would be sitting on his butt all day and wanted to get his blood pumping before they left Pine Hollow. He knew damned well by the time he got home, he would be way too tired to work out.

They made it to the Thatcher's warehouse by 6.45 am. Cody was inside and ready to roll the moment they arrived. They discussed the plan and decided to hit the same diner in Flagstaff as they did last time on the way to grab some breakfast. Same instructions as before for Rex. Ride ahead and report back anything that didn't look right. Keep Clay and Cody out of trouble by any means necessary.

As they made their way through the early morning streets of Pine Hollow, Clay noticed a very nice large house up on the hill that basically looked down over the entire town.

"Hey, nice house," Clay commented.

"You know who owns that house?" asked Cody with a sly smirk on his face.

"Nope. No clue," said Clay. "I know like 2 people in this town. How would I know who owns that place?"

"Go on, take one guess," said Cody, still with that annoying smirk on his face.

"Um.. yours?" asked Clay

"Mine? Why would that be my place?" asked Cody, almost offended.

"Well shit, man, I don't know. I told you I know two people in this town, and you still made me guess. So, of course, I just assumed it would be yours! Sheesh," Clay replied.

"Oh, come on, man, that makes no sense. Why would I be working for Dan if I owned that pad?" asked Cody.

"Yeah, I guess I didn't think of that," Clay replied. 'Well, I am all out of ideas then."

"Geez, buddy, I basically told you who owns it," said Cody, shaking his head.

Clay racked his brains to try and think of who Cody had mentioned. *Nina? Nope.* He was out of ideas.

"Damn, man, I already told you. I only know about 2 people in this town," Clay replied.

'Yes, and one of those two people owns that house. C'mon, man, think!"

Clay thought for a moment. If Nina lived there, why would she have that small house with Samantha? That made no sense.

"I give up. Just tell me," said Clay, sick of playing guessing games with Cody.

"Damn, son, I basically already told you the answer. Dan! Your boss and mine! Dan Thatcher," Cody explained, seemingly amused by the notion.

"Ah, okay, cool," Clay replied, not really sharing Cody's amusement on the subject.

The rest of the drive to Flagstaff was uneventful, and when they pulled into the Diner's parking lot, they easily spotted Rex's bike. They assumed he was already inside and looking for a table for them.

They ate breakfast in silence until Clay broke it.

"Man, I saw this huge house overlooking the entire town at the top of the hill today."

"Oh yeah. I saw that one too. Imagine owning that? Think of the parties we could have!" Rex replied.

"Yeah! That would be wild," Clay replied. "Guess who owns it?"

Rex thought for a minute. If Clay was asking him, it must be someone they both knew. Considering they knew about 3 people in town, it wasn't going to be hard to figure out.

"Hmm, let me think," Rex replied. Meanwhile, Cody stopped eating and stared at Rex, awaiting his answer.

"Hmm, I'm gonna go out on a limb here. I guess Dan?" said Rex.

'Ding ding ding! We have a winner," Cody exclaimed.

'Damn, got it in one," Clay replied. "How did you guess it was him?"

Rex thought for a moment. Whatever he said at the table here, right now, there was a good chance that it would get reported back to Dan.

'Well, cuz it seems Dan is a man about town. A mover and shaker, so to speak. So it would make sense for a guy like that to have a nice place, yeah?"

"Wow, I didn't even think of that," Clay replied 'You're so right."

Rex kept his eyes on Clay as they talked, but out of his peripheral vision, he noticed that Cody approved of Rex's answer.

Cody paid for their breakfast, and they continued their road trip to Las Vegas. As per the last ride, Rex rode ahead and checked in with Clay every thirty minutes. Rex was glad to be out on the open highways of Northern Arizona, but he was starting to get bored with the task at hand. He would rather be on the run with his club brothers as opposed to running security for some douchebag drug dealer. He let his mind wander as he rode, imagining cowboys on a cattle run in the old west.

The ride into Las Vegas was uneventful. Same drill as last time. Pull up at the suburban home. Cody runs to the front door. They i.d. him, and he returns to the florist van. Then, they go around the block and down the back alley to be ushered into the rear of the property.

Rex noticed this time they had a different guy on gate duties, but the dude looked just as sketchy as their last gatekeeper. Rex wondered if he was armed. He assumed so, although he didn't see a holster on the douchebag. Chances are, a guy like that would just shove his pistol right into his waistband.

The rear door of the house opened, and the same two guys who had bought boxes out for Cody last time stepped out and greeted them. Rex remembered them ignoring him last time, so he thought, fuck it, not making that mistake again. He sat on his bike as the two dealers and Cody worked quickly to bring the stack of U-haul boxes out and loaded them into the small waiting van.

After loading up their van, Cody made some small talk with the two guys. Rex couldn't make out what they were saying, but it seemed fairly civil, so he kind of zoned in and out. Just keen to get back on the road and back to Pine Hollow before nightfall.

And just like that, they were off again. Gatekeeper douchebag dragged the rear gates open and eyeballed both Rex and the Van as they made their departure, heading back down the suburban alley to the main road again.

Rex rolled through the suburban streets, heading towards the freeway on the ramp that would take them back to Arizona. Now that the van was loaded full of illegal contraband, he kept his eyes on a swivel. Slowing at each intersection, searching for anyone who looked like an undercover cop. He also kept an eye out for marked cop cars. Checking in with Clay the entire time, they traversed the suburban roads of Las Vegas. So far, so good.

They all made the on-ramp for the South Bound freeway home, and Rex hung up. He would call back if he noticed anything or anyone suspicious. Traffic heading into Vegas was noticeably more busy than traffic heading out of the city at this time of the day. *Good* thought, Rex. *Let them deal with it.*

Rex had to admit he did like this part of the 93 Freeway. Long, slow bends on the road, with picturesque views as far as the eye could see. He recalled somewhere his dad telling him that the opening scenes for the original Planet of the Apes movie (the 1960s one with Charlton Heston) were filmed in Northern Arizona. They made his heart soar with pride. To the Hollywood producers, Northern Arizona looked like the end of the world. Maybe this is what the beginning of the world looked like, too? Northern Arizona for the beginning and the end. Made sense to him.

Rex realized he needed to piss. Up ahead was one of his favorite stops, "Gus's Really Good Fresh Jerky." He speed-dialed Clay and told him they needed to pull over when they got to Gus's. Clay, who pretty much always thought with his stomach that it was a great idea, advised Cody to make sure they pulled in when they reached Gus's Jerky store.

Rex took a piss, then started checking out the food options at Gus's when Clay and Cody walked in.

"Good call, bro; this stuff is the bomb," Cody declared, walking into the jerky store.

With Clay hitting the bathroom, Rex bought sodas and bags of jerky for him and Clay. As far as he was concerned, Cody could buy his own damn jerky.

Rex wanted to eat before they got back on the highway. Both Clay and Cody could munch on their jerky as they drove, but he couldn't, so he made the most of their short break by the side of the highway.

When Clay exited the bathroom, Rex held up his purchases. The two friends had known each other for so long that Clay automatically knew what it meant. No need to buy food and drink; I have you covered.

Clay followed Rex outside, where Rex handed him a soda and a bag of Gus's jerky.

'Thanks, man, I'll get you next time," Clay replied.

'I know you're good for it, don't worry," Rex replied to Clay's offer.

"You know it." Clay smiled as he took a bite of the delicious jerky.

Cody joined them all business. "5 minutes, boys, and then we leave. We got deadlines to meet."

For some reason, Rex thought that was hilarious. Since when did drug dealers care about schedules? Usually, if you wanted what they had, you had to sit around and wait for them to turn up on their own damn time. Never early, always kept you waiting. *Fuck this guy* thought Rex. *I don't like him or Dan Thatcher.*

Rex tossed his empty soda bottle into the trash. He wiped his hands down on his jeans and pulled on his battered leather riding gloves. The bladder is emptied, hydrated, and has a full belly. It was time to roll.

Clay took his remaining jerky and soda and jumped back into the small passenger van. Cody got in the driver's seat, looked over at Rex, and nodded. The intent was clear. Time to go. Lead the way.

Rex started up his Harley. Nothing. Wtf? It was working fine 10 minutes ago. He tapped the gas tank. Nope. Still plenty of fuel. What now? He tried the engine again, but still nothing.

Rex honked. Hurry up, asshole. That's what that honk told Rex. He started his scoot again, but still nothing. Had the engine gremlins gotten into his ride as he was in the store? It made no sense. He waved over at Clay, Shaking his head and shrugging his shoulders. Something is wrong with my bike, he conveyed.

He put the kickstand down and got off his bike. He started checking the wiring on his starter. All good. Checked his battery connections. All good. What the hell was wrong with his damn scoot?

Cody angrily honked his horn again. Rex looked back at him and shrugged. Honking the horn wasn't going to help him troubleshoot any faster. He contemplated checking his spark plugs, maybe checking the gaps on them.

Rex pulled up alongside him.

'What's the holdup?" he shouted.

"Bike won't start," Rex shouted back.

'Well fuck, we can't wait for you, bro. You're just going to have to catch up," Cody shouted.

Rex was furious. "But...." he started to say

"Call Clay when you are on the move again. See ya!" Cody shouted before peeling out of the carpark, sending gravel and small stones into the air.

What a prick, thought Rex, shaking his head in disgust. The code of the road always said you don't leave a brother behind. *Asshole*

CHAPTER 23

Nina had slept in. It was a rare day off for her. Despite some people thinking that if you manage a bar, it's a 24-hour party, it sadly wasn't the case. Perhaps if you are 21 and just a bartender, maybe... but being the manager meant a lot more work had to go into your job than just turning up, "looking hot," and slinging drinks. Ordering booze, keeping track of food supplies, dealing with the bookkeeper, and managing staff never ended. It was like playing a game of whack-a-mole. As soon as you dealt with one problem, there were two more to deal with.

It was nice to wake up without a hangover, too. Technically, in most establishments, the boss didn't want the staff drinking on the job, but most people did. Even if it just meant sipping one beer all night long. However, if you were a female bartender in a town full of horny farmers and cowboys, if they wanted to drink with you, then well, you had to drink. Sure, you earned more tips, but some mornings, waking up with your mouth as dry as the Sonoran desert and your brain feeling like someone had embedded an axe in your skull, she wondered if it was all worth it.

Her mind went back to Clay, the outlaw biker. He was different, especially from the majority of the guys in Pine Hollow. He was quiet. He chose his words carefully. He wasn't a loudmouth. He seemed to contemplate things before speaking. She liked that about him.

They had made out when they had gone for their walk after the picnic. But that was it. She wanted to take it slow with him. After all, she was the queen of bad decisions and poor judgment, especially when it came to men. She thought back to some of her serious long-term relationships. There had been the cheating guy who fucked all her friends. The violent guy who smashed up all her possessions, numerous nights in Phoenix where he came home blind, drunk, and violent, she would have to flee in the night to a motel to protect herself.

The married guy. When she first moved to Pine Hollow, she thought she had found the perfect man, but later, she found out that he was married with kids. If Nina had known that beforehand, she would have never gotten involved with him. The creep. When she went to inform the wife, she realized the poor woman was pregnant with yet another kid, and she backed out from telling the lady.

Back to Clay. Clay lived in Tucson. Would she want to follow him there? Could she get him to stay in Pine Hollow? Wouldn't he be bored in a mountain town like this? What did she know about him? He wasn't married, and he didn't have kids. Well, that put him ahead of 98% of the males in Pine Hollow already.

Maybe he could move in with her after Samantha moved to Phoenix. Despite not being her daughter, she did her best to raise Samantha on her own ever since her mother died. How odd, really. She was raising a teenager on the promise of her dying best friend, and Clay was here attempting to deliver a motorcycle for a dying best friend, too. Maybe it was fate for them to be together? What was she thinking? They hadn't even slept together yet, and here she was, making plans for their future together.

Nina figured it was time to get out of bed, stop daydreaming, and take on the day. She had a house to clean and groceries to get before her work week started again. She would call Clay later and see how his day was going.

CHAPTER 24

R ex was just about to start checking for blown fuses when he noticed his kill switch was in the "off" position. No wonder his scoot wasn't starting. What the heck? Amateur mistake. It's a big-time amateur error. He hadn't made that mistake in over 20 years of riding. Had he done this? He didn't think so. It had been a long, long time since he had made a mistake as stupid as this.

When he pulled up, there were some kids out in front of Gus's Jerky playing by a minivan. Had one of them touched his bike? He doubted it. Besides, usually, when kids mess with a man's bike, they push and pull everything out of order. He very much doubted it.

That left only Cody. Had Cody done this? He couldn't prove it in a court of law, but he seemed like the logical choice. Why though? Just to fuck with him? What purpose did that serve?

He cursed himself for not noticing it earlier. That said, with Cody honking his horn like that, it was hard to think clearly and logically. How much of a head start did they have on him? 15 minutes? 20?

He texted Clay 'On my way."

Just as he was about to pull out of the car park for Gus's Jerky, his phone went off. It had to be Clay. He looked down at the screen. "On the 40 heading East."

Okay, so they were not that far away. He could catch them. He kicked his hawg into gear and took off out of the carpark, heading south towards the I-40 Freeway. Playing catch-up was a lot more fun than riding ahead, as he could ride as fast as he wanted, weaving in and out of the afternoon's traffic.

His adrenalin surged through his body when he passed between a slow-moving Walmart semi and a line of cars in the overtaking lane with a slow-moving car in the lead. If he had made one wrong move at this speed, he would have ended up under the semi's wheels. The slipstream created between the heavy-duty semi and the line of cars shook his bike, but he just laughed. Rex shook his head at the guy holding everyone up in the fast lane; people like that should just stay in the slow lane and wait. The fast lane was originally designed to overtake someone and swing back into the right-hand lane. Not for Sunday driving. Just for a moment, he almost felt sorry for those poor souls stuck behind the slowing-moving culprit but then figured, what the hell, nothing stopping them from getting a bike, too.

Within minutes, he made it to the ramp for the Eastbound 40. Heading west would have taken him into Needles, California (where they filmed a bunch of scenes for that 70's classic trucking movie Convoy) and then on to Los Angeles. Part of Rex wished he was heading West instead of East. In fact, he still had a couple of chicks in the Hollywood area he could call at any time to hang out.

The East Bound I-40 Freeway climbed, then twisted and turned. This was actually more enjoyable than riding ahead and keeping pace with the little Florist's van. Just as Rex was in the process of climbing a large hill, his phone went off. He looked down. It was Clay. He hit accept, but as soon as he did, the call cut out. Problems? Unusual for Clay to be calling him. They probably decided to pull over at some truck stop and let him know.

As soon as he crested the hill, he noticed a highway patrol cop car with its Cherries and Berries on. Fuck. That must be why Clay was calling him. So this ride wasn't all smiles and easy miles. He was going to have to do something. But what? If the cops searched the van, they were fucked. Rex racked his brains as he tried to remain focused on the road. He would have to fight the cop or something to give the boys a chance to get away. He hadn't been in trouble with the law for a good 15 years and groaned at the thought of being held in jail. Attending bail hearings. Paying through the nose for lawyers. Playing nice until you cleared probation. He swore years ago to try to play nice and avoid any more jail time.

What was the saying the old timers used to drum into their heads when they were prospects? Image and Action! That was it. Basically, what the O.G.s were telling them was not to rock the image if you can't handle the action. He had to do something.

He blipped down in gears to reduce speed and came up behind the cop car. He parked a good 50 yards away. Just as he was about to shut down his bike, he saw a nice softball-sized rock by the side of the road. He had an idea. He left his bike rumbling away to itself and picked up the rock. In stealth mode, he crept closer to the cop car. He could see the lone cop leaning into Clay's side of the van, asking them questions. He was distracted. Good. That would give Rex the precious moments he needed to do what he was gonna do.

He coiled his right arm back like he was about to pitch for the New York Yankees. At the top of his lungs, he shouted, "Fuck the cops," and with full force, pitched the rock right through the rear windows of the cop car. All hell broke loose. As he ran back to his waiting bike, he could hear the cop shouting 'What the actual fuck??" Rex braced himself for a bullet in the back that never came. He jumped on his bike, kicked it into gear, and was about to take off when he thought I couldn't head east. I will ride right into him. Instead, he swung his bike around and rode against traffic riding West in the eastbound lane.

No way will the cop follow him this way. The cop had kicked on his siren and was now on the other side of the I-40, giving chase. Shit. Rex hadn't expected the trooper's reaction time to be so fast. Cars honked at him as he dodged traffic, going 70 miles an hour. One wrong move at this speed, and you were going to wish you had gone down in a hail of bullets back there by the side of the road.

Soon, as Rex saw a clearing, he switched to the correct side of the freeway. Now, he was in the Westbound lanes heading West. He looked back; law enforcement was back there. He still had some time, but that cop car wasn't going to give up the chase anytime soon. Maybe if he had a sports bike, he could outrun the cop, but not on his cruiser. Besides, what was the one thing his old man used to drop into his head? No matter how fast you think, you can ride. You can't outrun a police radio. No doubt this cop had called ahead and was requesting backup from any free units in the area. He had to think of something fast.

He took the Kingman exit that led to the 93 South. The road signs warned him of going 35mph coming off the freeway. He took the turn at 60 miles but could feel his tires barely gripping the road. Any faster, and he would be on the low side for sure. Not good.

Passing Kingman, heading south, he desperately looked for somewhere to pull off and hide. He checked his mirrors. Just as he figured, the cop car was still chasing him. Some of these troopers were relentless.

His bike shook as he pushed it harder and faster. Finally, he saw it: an off-ramp for some small country town. He blipped his throttle as he geared down, consciously aware if he took the turn too fast, the cops would be peeling him off the pavement.

He made the turn and, on instinct alone, decided to turn left and not right towards the small town. Up ahead was an underpass for the 93 freeway, and on his left was a storm drain that was big enough to get his bike into. He stomped on his rear brake and skidded hard. He managed to ride his bike deep into the drain, all the while hoping there were no rattlesnakes using it as a home. His bike barely fit, and he had to clamber off the back of the bike to get off it. Pulling off his helmet, he crept back to the entrance to the drain system. Right as he did, a cop car drove by at high speed. He had made it. Just.

Rex was suspicious; knowing police procedures, they would probably backtrack at some point. He had to do something. He stuck his head out of the storm drain and looked for some brush or something to hide him and his scoot. There was some measly scrub off to his left, the same direction the cop car had gone, but he doubted it would be sufficient to hide him and his bike. Nope, not good enough.

He looked over to the right. He wasn't keen on leaving the tunnel, expecting the highway patrol to swing by at any moment. He took off his club vest, laid it over his bike seat, and returned to the drain entrance. There was a pile of trash over to the right, and perhaps there was something in there he could use. He gingerly stepped out onto the road, fearing at any second, the cops would light him up with sirens and lights. It was probably only 50 feet away from the storm drain entrance, but it felt like 50 miles.

He made it to the pile of trash and quickly sifted through it. To Rex's eyes, it seemed like a road crew had come along, cleaned up all the trash along the side of the road, and left it here for collection at a later date. A few bags of trash, soda cups, and juice bottles. A bunch of random-sized pieces of wood. Then he saw it. An old traffic sign. Sheet metal. Perfect!. He grabbed the metal sign, which was nearly 6 feet long; the last thing he needed was to shred his fingers with it. Moving quickly, he carried/dragged it across the road and back to the entrance of the storm drain. Height-wise, it was perfect, but wise, not so much. He had to drag it in on an angle to get it to fit. It worked, though, and that's all that matters.

Rex sat down beside his bike. He was now pretty much submerged in darkness. Above the top of the old street sign, some light shined in, but about 5% of what was moments beforehand. He figured he would wait until dark, and then it would be safe to come out and make it back to Pine Hollow. He hoped that his actions had given Cody and Clay ample opportunity to get away. He would wait awhile, then text Clay and double-check.

As he sat in the dingy tunnel, he thought of going back to elementary school. One of the kids in his class, Barry Corrigan, had run away from home at the age of 10 and had lived in a cave on the outskirts of Tucson. Rumors were he would steal candy bars from grocery stores to survive. He had been shocked by that story at the age of 10, but now, thinking about it as a fully grown adult, it was even worse. The level of fear poor Barry must have felt would have been terrifying. Tucson, after all, had rattlesnakes, bobcats, and coyotes. Not only that, you had to watch out for child molesters and the police. Barry's home life must have been pretty bad to have taken such measures. This wasn't a case of not getting a new Star Wars action figure and storming out of the house in a hissy fit. It must have been something very serious. At that point, Rex remembered Barry's father. A ruddy red face with broken blood vessels all over his nose. All the signs of a hard drinker. He probably beat Barry and his sister every time he got wasted. Sad. He hoped that Barry would get his life together after that and didn't end up doing a long prison stretch.

As he sat in the dark thinking about 10-year-old Barry, he heard a chopper overhead. Was that for him? He wasn't about to come out and check. Really though? A helicopter for a broken back window? Surely not.

He strained to listen some more and swore he heard a squad car cruising by. He could hear the squawk of the police band radio. Or did he? Perhaps his mind was playing tricks on him? He mentally braced himself for a bunch of cops with guns drawn ripping away the flimsy street sign and screaming at him to 'Show me your hands," but it didn't come.

Rex wasn't prepared to leave the safety of his hiding spot just yet. Some Dudley Do-right cop could still be cruising the area, determined to catch him. He sat back down and waited. And waited. Somewhere along the way, he must have passed out as he woke up to his phone buzzing in his vest pocket. He pulled it out in the darkness and checked. A text from Clay.

"u ok?"

He texted back, "Yes, u?"

"Home now – all good," was the reply he got from Clay.

"Okay, cool," Rex replied. He checked his phone, and it was after 9 PM. *Shiiitt, How long had he been asleep?* Didn't matter; he felt fairly certain the cops had probably stopped looking for him by now. Just to be sure, he took off his riding vest and turned it inside out before putting it back on. It looked ridiculous, but at least his club colors were not showing. Rex knew a lot of cop cars these days had rear cameras as well as front-facing ones. He had no idea how much (if any footage) of him that they got. Chances were not much, as he was a decent distance away, but he didn't feel like taking any chances. He grabbed the street sign, dragged it out of the drain, and left it on the sidewalk. He got back to his bike and realized he was going to have a problem walking it back out. It was one thing going in, but a whole other thing to get it back out. He contemplated crawling over it and pushing it backward by the handlebars but ended up mounting his bike and doing a weird duck walk waddle to get it out of the tight-fitting tunnel. Once again, Rex felt like, at any moment, cop cars would descend on both sides of the underpass and draw guns on him, but no one came. Regardless, he stayed on high alert until he was back on the I-40 heading East. If he had known of another way to get back to Pine Hollow, he would have taken it.

He rode the speed limit all the way East on the 40 just in case Highway patrol were still looking for him. He rode right past Flagstaff without incident. He kept his head on a swivel, and his eyes scanned ahead for any patrol cars on the road, too. Rex was convinced they would pounce on him out of nowhere at any given moment.

Finally, he reached the Hopi Drive exit, which would get him back on the I-77 heading South. He let out a huge sigh of relief once he was on the 77, and a lot of tension left his body. It surprised him how on edge he had been, but again he understood why. It had been so long since he had run afoul of law enforcement, and he really didn't want to fall back into the pattern of being in and out of jail again. He was beyond that now. Well, at least, so he hoped.

By the time he got to their hotel in Pine Hollow, he was beyond exhausted. He entered their room, but there was no sign of Clay. He assumed he was at the bar, probably drinking with Nina. He showered and got into bed, then texted Clay, "I'm back. Heading to sleep. TTYL." He switched his phone to silent and turned out the light. He wouldn't even wait for a reply from Clay, and he was just too tired.

That night, he had weird dreams; Barry Corrigan was in that cave in Tucson, 10 years old, scared, and alone. Somewhere before dawn, he was aware of Clay coming in. Was it 2 am? 5 am? He didn't know or care. His bro was back safe, and that was all that mattered. Screw Cody, Screw Dan Thatcher, and his crooked sheriff brother. He just wanted to get Samantha her rightful motorcycle and go home. He passed back out into a deep sleep again.

CHAPTER 25

Rex woke up and checked his phone. One missed call. Spike, the Phoenix president of the Steel Reapers Motorcycle Club. He looked over. Clay was fast asleep. It was 10 am. Rex dragged himself out of bed, took a piss, brushed his teeth, and washed his face. He then pulled on his jeans, grabbed his boots, and headed outside. Let Clay sleep it off, he figured.

He dialed Spike's number. It rang a couple of times before he picked up.

"Hey, Rex – how's it going?" Spike asked.

"All good, how's about you?"

"Yeah, busy man, busy," Spike replied 'What town are you in again? Some Northern Arizona town, right?"

"Yeah, Pine Hollow," Rex explained.

"Where the hell is that?' asked Spike

"It's a small town between Holbrook and Snowflake," Rex replied.

"What the? Where are those towns?" asked Spike, somewhat confused.

"You know Show Low, right?" asked Rex

'Yeah, I know, Show Low," Spike replied.

'We are just past Show Low, same highway, the 77; keep heading North until you pass Snowflake."

"Ok, so somewhere in the White Mountains, I guess?" asked Spike.

"Yeah, pretty much. It's super nice up here. You wouldn't even think you are in Arizona," said Rex.

"Sounds cool," said Spike

"So what's up?" asked Rex

"Oh yeah, that's why I'm calling you," said Spike. "We have finished Clay's van repairs, and we should be done by the weekend with his hawg."

"Oh shit, that's great news. He's sleeping right now, but I will let him know when he wakes up," Rex replied.

"No problems, brother. You boys gonna come down to collect, or so we bring 'em up to you?" Spike asked.

Rex thought for a moment. Did he really want to ride nuts to butts with Clay for a few hours all the way to Phoenix? Probably not.

"Hey, maybe bring it up here. If it's not too much trouble?" asked Rex.

"Hmm, I could do it with a few days out of town. Where are you boys staying?" asked Spike.

"We got a cheap motel on the outskirts of town; I should be able to score a couple more rooms, I reckon," said Rex.

"Very cool; I will check with my guys and see who wants to take a road trip for a couple of days and get back to ya, okay?" Spike replied.

"Awesome, beers on me when ya get here," said Rex

'Thanks, brother, appreciated. Hey, I gotta run. Talk soon, bye," said Rex

'Ok, later, bro," said Rex, hanging up his phone.

Spike and the Phoenix boys were solid dudes. Rex respected that.

CHAPTER 26

Rex returned to their motel room to find Clay's bed empty and the bathroom door closed. He could hear the shower going inside the bathroom. Good! Clay was up and about, finally. As soon as he was ready, they headed down Main Street to their breakfast spot. It was nearly 11 am. For his life, he could not remember if their diner stopped serving breakfast at 11 am or 12. Who knew? No doubt, in this town, it would be 11 am. Give it 5 years, and the concept of an "All Day Breakfast" would come to the sleepy town of Pine Hollow. One could only hope.

Clay greeted him. He looked clean and rested well.

"Hey bro, how you doing?" he asked Rex.

"Yeah, all good, thanks; I'm starving. Hurry up and get ready so we don't miss out on breakfast," he told Clay.

"Oh, breakfast! Yeah!" said Clay. "I'm in desperate need of some coffee, too."

"Yeah, same bro; hurry up."

5 minutes later, they were making their way down the main street towards their diner.

By the time they were seated and served coffee and iced water, it was already 11 am. Sure enough, breakfast was over. They begged their waitress to speak to the cook and make an exception for them. Luckily, he was in a good mood and agreed.

"I spoke to Spike earlier," Rex told Clay over coffee.

"Oh yeah? Any news on my van?" asked Clay.

"Yeah, actually, it's done!" said Rex

"No shit, very cool," Clay smiled 'And what about my bike?"

"They'll have that finished by the end of the week," Rex told him.

'Cool, so when do you wanna ride down and collect it?" asked Clay

'Well, Spike and the boys might bring it up, bro. Save us a journey," Rex explained.

'Ahh, nice, very cool of them," Clay replied.

"Yeah, I agree. They kinda wanna see the town, too," said Rex

"Awesome. So do you know when?" asked Clay.

"Probably early next week," said Rex. "He's checking to see who is down for a road trip."

"Nice!" said Rex 'I like those Phoenix boys."

"Yeah, me too," Rex replied. "So what happened yesterday after I smashed that cop's back window?"

"Oh, it worked a treat. He took off after you like a bat out of hell," laughed Clay. "Cody didn't wait around. As soon as he left, we raced back home."

"Ok, good," Rex replied.

"Yeah, Cody was impressed you stepped up," said Clay 'He even raved about it to Dan."

Rex shook his head. "Whatever it takes to get the job done, eh?"

'Yeah, man, so what did they do? Chase you all the way back to Vegas or something?" asked Clay.

"Nah, I circled back through Kingman and found a place to hide. Took a nap and came home about 10 PM."

'Oh shit, that's kinda awesome," Clay exclaimed.

"Eh, it was overrated, trust me. I could have done without it," shrugged Rex.

"Oh well, two more runs, and we will get the bike back. Ya know?" said Clay

"Yeah, true," Rex replied. "So what about you?"

'What do you mean what about me?" asked Clay

"After you did the run, you went out, right?' asked Rex

"Yeah! How did you know?" asked Clay

'Cuz you weren't home when I got back, duh," said Rex.

"Oh, I went and hung out with that Nina chick," explained Clay.

"Yeah, figured as much," said Rex. "How's that all going?"

"Good, good, actually," said Clay with a sly smile on his face.

"You dirty dog," teased Rex.

"Nah, Nah, nothing like that yet, bro. Just making out and stuff," Clay explained.

'Sure, sure. I believe ya. Millions would not," Rex replied.

The waitress brought their breakfast plates over. Rex quickly scanned both plates so that Clay wouldn't start picking at his plate again.

He just started on his scrambled eggs when he felt his phone go. He put down his fork and checked his phone. A message from Dan: 'Can you be here at 2 PM today?"

Rex wiped his fingers on his napkin and typed back 'Sure, see u then."

"Hey, we gotta meet Dan this afternoon," Rex explained.

"Another run already?" asked Clay.

"Who knows?" said Rex. "I guess we shall soon find out."

"Yeah, you're right," Clay replied.

CHAPTER 27

The boys went back to their motel and lay on their respective beds watching TV. Around 1.30 PM, they walked down the main street towards Dan's warehouse. They arrived and rang the buzzer on the door.

The original dude they met on that first night, along with Dan and Cody, answered the door. Rex realized he had no clue of this guy's name.

"Hey, I'm Rex," he said, sticking his hand out for the cowboy to shake.

The redneck looked at it like he had shit on the palm of his hand. Then, finally, he stuck his hand out to shake Rex's.

"Hey, I'm Keith," the man replied.

"This is Clay," said Rex. Clay stuck his hand out and shook Keith's hand as well.

"This way, fellas. Dan is waiting on you." Keith led Clay and Rex back through the warehouse to Dan's office. As they passed through aisles of boxed products, Rex spied Samantha's chopper, sitting there untouched. A relief.

Keith knocked on Dan's door and opened it.

"The bikers are here," he announced.

"Send 'em in," Dan replied.

Keith showed Clay and Rex into Dan's office.

"You need me to stick around?" Keith asked.

"Nah, all good," Dan replied.

"Hey, boys' Dan greeted Clay and Rex. "Take a seat."

Rex and Clay grabbed seats and sat down across the desk from Dan.

"So, what's up?" asked Rex

"Yeah, so Cody told me about your work yesterday, Rex," said Dan. "Good job."

"No problem. That's what I am paid to do, right?" Rex replied.

"Yeah, true, but that was quick thinking, and I appreciate it," Dan explained.

"No worries, man. All part of the service," said Rex.

"Well, I want to give you both a $1000 bonus for yesterday," Dan continued. "I mean, if Cody and Clay had been caught, that would be a few hundred thousand dollars of product lost."

'Yeah, I figured as much," said Rex.

Dan got up from his desk and punched in the combination of his safe. On the angle Rex was on, he could see large stacks of cash and a couple of handguns. Dan fished around for a moment, grabbed some cash, and closed his safe.

He returned to his desk and counted out two stacks of $20 bills until he had reached a thousand each.

"Here you go, boys," he said, handing both of them a thousand dollars.

Clay reached over and grabbed him, then passed a stack over to Rex, too.

"Thanks, Bro," said Rex, grabbing his one thousand from Clay. "Much appreciated, Dan."

"My pleasure. You guys did good," Dan smiled.

'So let me ask you," said Rex. "Does this still mean we have to do two more runs to get back Clay's motorcycle?"

Dan thought for a moment, "Yes, a deal's a deal. Two more runs, and you will have earned that chopper."

"Ok, thanks," said Rex. "One more this week, right?"

Dan checked his computer. Rex assumed he was looking at a calendar or day planner.

"Yeah, this Thursday and..... next Monday. Okay?"

"Yeah, that's great. Thanks, Dan," said Rex. Clay nodded approvingly.

"Well, I gotta get on with some work. Thanks again for everything yesterday," said Dan 'Don't spend your bonus all at once, eh?

"Don't worry, we won't," Rex replied, getting up from his seat. "We will see you Thursday then."

"Thanks, Dan," said Clay, getting up and following Rex out the door to Dan's office.

As they left the warehouse, they saw Keith replacing the florist decals on the side of the van with decals for a local ice cream brand.

Smart thought Rex, *Just in case those highway patrol boys are looking out for a Florist's van.*

"Shall we hit the bar?" asked Clay.

Dan thought for a moment. "Sure, why not?"

"I'm buying," Clay announced, patting his vest pocket where he had put all his cash.

"Cool," said Rex, following Clay to the Dead Crow Saloon.

CHAPTER 28

Wednesday was a write-off. They both drank way too much the night before and ended up sleeping in. They missed breakfast at their diner but did manage to get a decent lunch out of them. Food was in their bellies, and a few pots of coffee were available, and both Rex and Clay started to feel fairly human again.

Once back at their motel, Clay got a text from Nina, wanting to hang out. Rex wanted to work on his scoot before the Vegas run on Thursday, so he spent the afternoon first adjusting his clutch cable, then working on the rest of his bike to make sure nothing had shaken loose from his last ride.

Clay still wasn't back at the motel by 5 PM, so Rex walked down to the local diner and bought a pizza to take back to his room. He ate half the pizza and watched TV while he waited for Clay to come back.

Next thing you know, it was morning, and his alarm was going off.

"Oh fuck turn that shit off," hollered Clay from his bed.

"Dude, time to get ready. We got a run today," Rex shouted, jumping out of bed and shutting off the alarm on his phone. By the time he got out of the shower, Clay was up and dressed. He looked like he hadn't slept.

"You good to go, bro?" Rex asked all concerned.

"Hey, I'm up, bro. I'm as good as I am gonna be," Clay grumbled.

Rex laughed. "That's what you get for going out on a school night."

"Fuck YOUUUUUUUUUUU," Clay replied, holding his head in his hands.

Rex dressed, and they rolled down the empty Main Street towards Dan's warehouse.

'So what did you get up to last night, you dirty bastard?" asked Rex as they rode.

"Oh, Nina took me to Flagstaff," Clay replied. "She took me to a place called The Cornish Pasty."

"What's that a burlesque joint or something?" Rex asked

"Nah, Nah, it's like an English pub-style place. A pasty is some British food. Pretty good. You were thinking of a pastie, what strippers were. YOU dirty bastard," teased Clay.

"Whatever," grumbled Rex as they entered the car park for Dan's warehouse. The florist van, now an ice cream truck, was waiting for them.

Clay jumped off the back of Rex's bike and went to grab Cody. Rex sat waiting, not anticipating any delays.

Moments later, Cody appeared with Clay. Cody locked the warehouse door and led Clay to the van. He nodded at Rex, but that was it. No cheery, "good morning," or any other words.

Perhaps he's not a morning person? Thought Rex to himself, slightly amused. Making sure they were in the van and ready to go, Rex led the procession out of the warehouse carpark, towards the main street, then Highway 77 North towards Flagstaff.

CHAPTER 29

The ride to Flag was uneventful. As was now their tradition, they stopped in town for breakfast. As they sipped coffee and waited for their food orders, Rex complimented Cody on the decal changes in their van.

"Hey man, nice move, swapping out the Florist decals for an ice cream brand. That was smart."

Cody stared at him for a minute, then replied, "Oh, you think just because we are from a small town, we aren't as smart as you big city folks?' he snapped.

'What the hell, man?" asked Rex. "I was giving you a damn compliment."

"Yeah, yeah," Cody groused.

"Look, we are from Tucson, not Chicago, LA, or Phoenix, bro, so chill."

"Yeah," added Clay, "Sheesh, people from Phoenix sneer at us for being podunk."

Cody continued to scowl as the waitress bought them their plates of eggs, bacon, home fries, and toast.

As Rex ate him, he decided he didn't like Cody either. He did not have as much hate for him as Dan or his evil brother Calvin, but he still vowed to keep this creep at arm's length for as long as he stayed in the town of Pine Hollow.

Cody paid their bill, and they filed for the car park out of the breakfast joint.

"Just ride ahead and phone it in, would ya?" Cody grumbled.

"Of course," Rex replied, refusing to let Cody's bad mood spoil his morning.

Rex fired up his Harley and tore out of the car park.

As Cody started up the little van, he turned to Clay and commented.

'What's up his ass?"

Clay kept his mouth shut and kept his eye on his phone for Rex's updates. 30 minutes further into their ride to Vegas, Cody asked Clay

"So, what's up with you and Nina then?"

"How do you know about that?" asked Clay, somewhat surprised.

"Dude, it's a small town. Everyone knows everyone's business," Cody explained.

"She's a cool chick," Clay replied.

"Well, keep ya wits about ya, buddy. Chick's like her cannot be trusted." Cody continued

"Thanks, I'll try and keep that in mind," said Clay, somewhat sarcastically.

Clay kept his eyes on the road as much as Cody did. Despite Rex riding ahead and looking out for them, a cop could easily enter the highway after Rex rode by, and they should stay vigilant at all times, not just when Rex calls it in.

They stopped on the 93 about an hour out of Vegas for a gas stop, piss stop, food stop and hydration. Clay was finally over his hangover and starting to feel human again.

"How you boys holding up? " Rex asked Clay and Cody once they exited their van.

"I'm actually feeling a lot better now," Clay replied. Meanwhile, Cody just stared at Rex.

Fuck that guy, thought Rex to himself. Rex ignored Cody's sour attitude and took in the view. He loved it out here, with open desert plains and mountains in the distance. He imagined being a cowboy in the early days of the Southwest and how that would have been. No gas stations, no cars, no cell phones. You and your wits against the elements.

After gassing up both the van and Rex's scoot, they went inside and looked at all the trinkets and knick-knacks the truck stop had to offer. There was some cool stuff here, and one day, Rex vowed to start a collection of roadside oddities he picked up on his travels.

The next hour into Vegas went smoothly; a couple of highway patrol cars out there, but they were ignoring both Rex and the "ice cream" van. Good. With the same drill as before, they pulled up at the suburban house. Cody got out, went to the front door, returned to the van, and pulled around back.

The same meth troll as last time worked the back gate looking bored and barely paying them any attention. It got Rex thinking about how many times a day this kid repeated this process. They probably supplied a bunch of dealers all over Nevada, Arizona, Utah, and Colorado, by the looks of things. No wonder they didn't want anyone going into their house and scoping it out. A sure invitation for robbery.

Two guys Rex had never seen before exited the back of the house, loaded up the ice cream van, and said something to Cody that Rex couldn't hear. He sat on his bike, waiting for the signal, finally getting a nod from Cody. He maneuvered his Harley around and waited for the meth boy to open the gate for them. Rex rolled out, looking both ways before heading back down the alley. He half expected to be swarmed by the DEA or local cops, but no one came for them.

On the way back south on US 93, they stopped off at Gus's Jerky to stretch their legs and have a quick break. Rex kept one eye on his bike the whole time, especially after the last time they stopped there. No kids are playing in the car park this time, and no Rex is hovering over his hawg, either. After 5 minutes, Cody nodded, but it was time to go.

"Okay, stay frosty on this one, Mister Biker man; this is the leg we got pulled over last time; we don't want a repeat of Monday's run if you know what I am saying," said Cody.

"You got it," said Rex, refusing to let Cody get to him.

He peeled out of the car park and rejoined the highway south, soon taking the on-ramp for the Eastbound 40. Rex kept his head on a swivel and looked out for speed traps. He called Clay every 15 minutes, reporting that the coast was clear.

After being spooked on their last run, they had decided earlier not to stop for food on the way back. Cody was confident that once they made the I-77 corridor, they would be safe. Rex had agreed to the plan but was starting to feel it, especially in his lower back and shoulders. He did his best to stay alert, but all he could think about was grabbing food and some beers back in Pine Hollow.

Somehow, they made it back with no harassment from law enforcement. Rex was shutting down his bike in the warehouse car pack when Cody and Clay pulled up.

"Hey, give us a hand bringing these boxes in, would ya?" asked Cody.

Rex didn't reply but left his helmet on his handlebars and went and helped load them in. With Clay and Cody, they made short work carrying the U-haul boxes into Dan's warehouse.

The other cowboy who was with Dan and Cody the first night Rex and Clay visited was there. He looked up as they entered and nodded.

"Everything go smoothly?' he asked Cody.

"Yeah, no issues today," Cody replied.

"Hey, I'm Steve," said the second cowboy, holding out his hand for Rex to shake. Rex took it and introduced himself, as did Clay. Steve then excused himself and disappeared further into the warehouse.

Dan shouted out from his office, "Hey Cody, is that you?"

"Yeah, we're back," Cody replied.

"Cool, can you send the bikers in?" he asked.

Cody looked back at Rex and Clay and gestured with his head for them to enter Dan's office.

The first thing Rex noticed walking in was that Dan seemed wired. The second thing he noticed was a tray with lines of white powder laid out on it. *Shit,* though, Rex, he's breaking the number one rule of any dealer, "Don't get high on your own supply."

"Oh hey guys," greeted Dan without looking up 'Have a seat."

Rex and Clay sat down.

"How did it go today?" asked Dan.

"Good, no issues, no cops," Rex replied.

"Oh shit, how rude of me. Do you want a line?" asked Dan, gesturing to the rows of white powder he had racked out on a tray on his desk.

"What is that? Coke?" asked Clay.

"Nah, Crystal," Dan replied, "It's good."

Rex never really messed with drugs; booze was his thing.

"Nah, bro, we're good. Thanks, tho," Rex said.

"Oh well, more for me then!" Dan replied happily.

"Enjoy," said Rex. "So we gotta get going. One more run on Monday, right?"

"What? Oh yeah, yeah. Monday, yeah, all good," Dan replied.

"And we get our chopper back? Correct?" asked Rex

Dan paused for a moment. Almost like he was looking straight through Rex and Clay

"Chopper? Oh, that motorcycle? Sure, yeah, sure, whatever," said Dan.

"Ok, great, we gotta get going. Thanks, Dan," Rex replied.

"Yeah, thanks," said Clay, getting up and exiting Dan's office.

They said goodbye to Steve and Cody as they exited the large warehouse.

'Wanna hit the bar?' asked Clay

Rex was more hungry than thirsty but then remembered they had a decent burger there.

'Yeah, sure, let's go," said Rex.

CHAPTER 30

Rex wanted to return his bike to the motel before getting drunk. He doubted there would be a booze checkpoint in Pine Hollow, but that said, he didn't want to give crooked cop Calvin and his cronies any excuses to take him to jail.

Clay walked to the Dead Crow Saloon, and Rex rode his scoot back to the motel, explaining to Clay that he would meet him in the bar at 15.

Rex parked his bike at the motel and walked back down the main street to hit the saloon. This little town was starting to grow on him. Not that he could ever see himself living here, but he appreciated the fact that you had to "slow yourself down" to adapt to living here versus in a major city like Phoenix.

When he entered the Dead Crow Saloon, Clay was, sure enough, sitting at the bar chatting with Nina. *Color me shocked,* thought Rex. He ordered a beer and a shot, plus a burger and fries. He definitely felt he earned a drink today but wanted to line his stomach with food before any more drinks. He had been caught out before drinking on an empty stomach, and it never ended well for Rex.

After scarfing down their burgers, Rex ordered them another round of beers and shots. Nina had to go up to the other end of the bar and attend to some regular customers.

'Hey, remember that time Eli fought that Mixed Martial Arts fighter?" Rex asked Clay, thinking back to the old days.

"No, when was that?" asked Clay

Rex thought back – it was after their charity run to Florence prison, not Florence, Colorado, but Florence, Arizona, sandwiched between Tucson and Phoenix. The club did it every year to remind their brothers behind the wire they were not forgotten.

"Hmm, it had to be the early 2000s, Clay," said Rex. "It was after our annual prison run to Florence."

"Umm, okay, we did a bunch of those," Clay replied.

"Yeah, yeah, I know," said Rex. "Anyways, after the ride, you, me, and Eli had to go to Walmart."

"Why would we need to go to Walmart in Florence, of all places?' asked Clay

"Dunno, man; maybe Eli needed to grab something? Who knows? That's not important," Rex said.

"Okay,"

'Anyways, it was just when Mixed martial arts and UFC were getting popular," Rex continued.

"I remember those days," said Clay

"Yeah, so you and I are following Eli around Walmart, and this dude approaches us."

"Okay, I think I remember that," said Clay 'He kept wanting to fight us cuz of our riding vests, right?"

'That''s the guy. He pulled the usual. 'You guys think you're tough cuz you belong to a gang, BS," said Rex.

'Yep, even after we tried to explain we are a riding club, not a gang, he wouldn't leave it alone," said Clay

'Ain't it always the same story?' asked Rex. "Anyways, Eli could already see where this was going and warned the guy twice to let it go, even turning his back on him and walking off."

"Yeah, that's right," said Clay

'So the guy keeps following us, and Eli has finally had enough," Rex continued.

"So he stops and gets in the jerk's face, right?" asked Clay

"Yeah, pretty much. What Eli didn't know is that this guy had been training in Mixed martial arts, which was pretty much a new fighting style at that time," said Rex

"Yeah, that's right! Back then, it was pretty much unheard of," said Clay.

"So they start scrapping, and at first, this dude is getting the best of Eli. Eli can't believe it," said Rex 'He was used to boxing and wrestling, not this style of fighting."

"So true, I guess that's where the guy thought he had the advantage over Eli," said Clay

"Yep, and Eli being Eli, he didn't want us to jump in," Rex continued.

'Yeah," Clay added

"So this guy is dominating Eli, and Eli can't figure out what the hell is happening. He has never fought a guy like that before," said Rex

'I remember that," said Clay

"So yeah, Eli gets free from this chokehold the douche bag had him in, jumps to his feet, the douche does the same, you know, squaring off for round two," said Rex

"That's right," said Clay

'So yeah, Eli knows he barely dealt with the shit bag when they were on the ground, looks oversees a shovel in the racks, pulls it off the shelf, and just cracks this loser over the head with it," said Rex

"And down he goes, lights out, douche bag," said Clay.

"Yeah, he was toast," said Rex. "That guy forgot one thing."

'What's that?" asked Clay

"Well, you can train all you want for the Octagon; that's great," Rex explained.

"Yeah, true," said Clay

"But the one thing he forgot," Rex continued, "Was that there was no referee in street fights. The only rule is to win."

'Yeah, so true. Anything goes," said Clay, raising his glass to toast Rex

'Fuck, I miss him, man. They don't make guys like Eli anymore," Rex commiserated.

"They sure don't," Clay replied. 'Hey, remember that time drinking at the Filthy Hogg in Phoenix?"

'Damn, bro, we were always drinking there when we rode up to Cowtown," Rex replied. "Which time?"

"We were still prospects and that you, I, and Eli walked in," Clay explained 'I forget which club that dude was in, but he walked up to Eli and told him Steel Reapers were not welcome in the bar."

"Oh yeah," laughed Rex, "I know where you're going with this."

"So yeah, Eli tells him. We go where we want. We do what we want. Then he turns his back on the guy and continues enjoying his drink."

"Damn, I remember it like yesterday," said Rex

"So douche bag from some club I can't remember taps Eli on the shoulder and threatens to throw him out," said Clay.

"Yeah, he wasn't even bothered by us. I guess cuz we were prospects or cuz we were so young," said Rex.

"Yeah, take yer pick," said Clay. "So Eli just looks at the guy and says, "Who's going to throw me out? You?"

"Haha," laughed Rex.

'So then the guy warns Eli that he is a black belt in Karate," said Clay

"Yeah. So ever so calmly Eli just gets up and head butts the guy unconscious," laughed Rex.

"Yeah. That always stuck with me. Neither of us had ever seen a head butt used in street fighting before, amazing." Clay stated.

"Yeah, and it also taught me that just cuz someone is a black belt in a martial art doesn't mean they will be an effective street fighter," Rex added.

'Yeah, that blew my mind," said Clay. "Before Eli, if someone told me they were a black belt, I wouldn't want to fight them."

"Yeah, same bro, same."

They spent the rest of the night drinking and sharing stories about the old days before their long, drunken walk down the main street back to their motel.

CHAPTER 31

Saturday was a write-off. Rex let himself sleep in. He tried to get up at sunrise, and his entire body was telling him to go back to bed, so he did.

Clay woke up around 12 PM and, after his shower, woke up Rex. Rex thought to himself, *It's funny when I wake up before him. I try to keep quiet and let him sleep in, but if Clay wakes before me, he has no qualms about waking me up.*

"Bro, bro. Hurry up and wake up. I'm starving." Clay shook Rex's body.

"Ugh, you fucker, gimme five minutes," Rex grumbled, getting out of bed and heading to the bathroom.

Once again, they were too late to prepare the breakfast menu. Rex made a mental note to come back and visit Pine Hollow in 10 years when some restaurant owner might have figured out "All-day breakfast." Instead, he settled on a grilled sandwich and a bunch of coffee.

'What do you wanna do for the rest of the day?' asked Clay between mouthfuls of bread.

"Dude, I'm gonna go back to the motel and watch TV," said Rex. "I am feeling really lazy today."

'Sounds good. Shall we hit the bar tonight, though?" asked Clay

'Sure, why not?" said Rex, not wanting to think that far ahead.

They spent the afternoon chilling in their motel room, mindlessly watching TV before hitting the Dead Crow Saloon that night. They took it easy on the beers as Nina had invited them to Sunday lunch with Samantha the next day.

Rex didn't feel too bad Sunday morning despite the amount of beers they eventually consumed the night before. He crept outside so as not to wake Clay and did his morning workout routine. He then basked in the sun until it hit 10 am. At that point, he decided to go wake up Clay so they could at least get breakfast before the diner stopped serving. Thinking about it, he was surprised they were even open on a Sunday in this small town.

After breakfast, they walked back up the main street to their motel.

'What time do we have to be over at Ninas and Samanthas?" asked Rex

"Ah, I think she said 2 PM?' Clay replied.

"You think?" asked Rex

"Yeah, man, c'mon, I was pretty wasted last night," Clay shrugged.

"Well, text her and confirm ya, dumbass," Rex replied.

"Yeah, good idea," said Clay, pulling out his phone and tapping in a message to Nina as they walked back.

Rex heard Clay's phone ping. He pulled it back out from his jean pocket.

"Yeah, 2 PM," said Clay after reading the message

"Okay, cool. I'm gonna work on my scoot until then, okay?" said Rex

"Damn, I wish I could work on my bike, too," said Clay. "I'm really missing it."

"Fuck man, I didn't even think of that," Rex replied. "Let me call Spike and see what day they can come up and drop your van and bike off."

"Thanks, brother. It is much appreciated," said Clay, patting Rex on the back.

Back at the motel, Clay went in to watch TV, and Rex grabbed his tool roll and went outside to tune his Harley. Just as he laid his tool roll out on the ground, his phone went. He grabbed it to see if it was worth answering. It was Spike, the president of the Phoenix chapter of the Steel Reapers.

"Hey brother – you saved me a call," said Rex, answering the phone.

"Oh yeah? Great minds think alike, eh?" asked Spike

"Yeah, they do. So, are you boys coming up or what? asked Rex

"Yeah, tomorrow," Spike replied. you

"Monday? Hm okay. We gotta do a run to Vegas, but we will be back early evening," explained Rex."After I hang up, I'll text you the motel address. I checked this morning. They still have plenty of rooms, and they're cheap too."

"Alright, cool," said Spike, "I'll text ya tomorrow and let ya know when we are en route, okay?"

'Yeah, sounds good," said Rex 'See ya soon. Oh, and Spike.."

"Yeah?" asked Spike

"Thanks for everything, man – we really appreciate it. You guys are true brothers," said Rex

"No worries, man. We got you covered," said Spike. "Good luck in Vegas, and see ya soon."

"Later, bro," said Rex, hanging up his phone.

CHAPTER 32

Rex finished tuning his bike and went back to wash up. At 1.45 PM, he gave Clay a ride over to Nina and Samantha's place.

Nina greeted them both at the door. Kissing Rex on the cheek and Clay on the lips. Rex made note of this.

Her small house smelt great.

"Wow, smells great. What ya cooking?" asked Clay

"I'm doing up my secret recipe, meatloaf," Nina replied. "It's Samantha's favorite."

"Yum, love meatloaf," said Clay. "What time lunch?"

Nina looked back into the kitchen at the clock. "About 15 minutes. Okay?'

"Awesome," said Clay

"Thanks, Nina," said Rex.

After lunch, the four sat around the dinner table.

"Damn, that was incredible," Rex complimented. "I've forgotten how superior home-cooked food is to restaurant food."

"Aww, thanks," Nina said

'Yeah, we've been eating out for so long now, that was great," said Clay. "Delicious, in fact."

"So we have a rule here," said Nina. "Whoever does the cooking doesn't have to do the cleaning up."

'Oh shit, I knew there was a catch," teased Rex. "C'mon Samantha, give me a hand loading the dishwasher."

'Dishwasher?" asked Nina. "You want to get loaded?"

'Huh?" asked Rex. It took him a second... "Oh wait, you don't have a dishwasher?"

"Nope, strictly old school here," Nina laughed. "Get to it, boys."

Rex looked at Clay and laughed, "Uhh, okay."

After Rex and Clay had finished cleaning up the mess in Nina's kitchen, she requested to have a word outside with Rex. He took a breath and thought to himself *Oh boy, here it comes. Some form of talk about Clay,* he was sure of it.

They stepped outside and away from Nina's house.

"So, what's up?' asked Rex.

"Gotta a favor I need to ask you," Nina declared.

"Sure, what do you need?" asked Rex.

"I wanna take Clay to Sedona this afternoon. Would you mind looking after Samantha for me?" she asked.

'What? Me? Babysit?" asked Rex, taken back by the request.

"Well, she's hardly a baby Rex," said Nina 'She practically looks after herself."

"Uh huh," Rex replied.

'Oh c'mon, please," begged Nina. "You can't be a hard ass all the time."

"Hey, I'm never a hard ass," joked Rex.

'Yeah, Yeah," Nina replied.

"Look, we got to be up at 6 am tomorrow for a run to Vegas, so do not keep him out late. Okay?" said Rex

"Ok, deal." Nina stuck her hand out to Rex like they were two old prospectors spitting in their palms and shaking on a claim. Rex shook her hand.

"Do not be late," he warned her.

"I won't' Nina pouted.

Ya better not be," Rex mocked, warning her, following Nina back inside her house.

Somewhere in the back of the house, Rex could hear Nina talking to Samantha.

He sat down on the couch and flicked on the TV as Nina hustled Clay out of there.

"Uh..back in a few, bro," Clay said as he was getting whisked out the front door of Nina's place.

"Have fun, bro," said Rex, more concerned about finding an interesting show to watch. "Don't forget to start early tomorrow. Last Vegas run if you get me."

"Oh shit. I had totally forgotten about that," said Clay

"Well, that's your reminder!' Don't come home drunk at 4 am," said Rex.

"Alright, gotta go," said Clay as Nina grabbed his arm and dragged him out the door. Rex shrugged better Clay than him. He figured Nina didn't get many opportunities to step out to look after a teenage surrogate daughter.

Rex found a TV show on Black Holes and the Cosmos that was somewhat interesting. Well, it held his interest much more than modern-day television shows did.

Eventually, Samantha wandered in, glued to her cell phone.

Typical teen, thought Rex to himself.

She sat on the other end of Nina's sectional couch, staring at her phone. From what Rex could see, she was just scrolling.

His TV show ended, and the announcer said the next show was about how the planets of the solar system formed. It was not his boat, but it sounded better than most of the other shows on TV, so he figured he would just stick with it.

"Oh god, I am so bored," Nina announced.

"Well, get off your damn phone and go do something," said Rex without thinking 'No wonder you are bored, just glued to your phone all day."

"There's nothing to do around here," whined Samantha.

"Sure, there's always stuff to do," said Rex, still watching TV.

"Like what?" huffed Samantha.

'Like going and hanging out with your friends," suggested Rex.

"I was doing that already!" Samantha declared.

"You went out this morning?" asked Rex

"So silly, I was checking out my friend's 'Toks,'" Samantha explained.

"Oh, my sweet summer child," Rex said, channeling his old grandma 'That's not hanging out with them."

'What is it then?' asked Samantha.

'That's looking at the photos or videos via your phone, silly," chided Rex.

"Look, take it from me," said Rex, realizing he was starting to sound like his Grandpa. "Get off your ass, get outside, and learn something new. Trust me, you will feel so much better if you do so."

'Like what?' asked Samantha.

"I dunno, not up for me to say, chuck a football around? Throw a Frisbee? Get some fresh air and sunlight, you know."

"No, I don't know," Samantha replied 'That's why I am asking you!'

Rex thought for a moment. He had no clue what teenage girls liked these days.

Well????" she asked

"I dunno, learn to ride a motorcycle or something," he said, almost immediately regretting his words.

'What? Really? No way! Would you teach me? Oh wow, so cool, Uncle Rex." Samantha tossed her phone down on the couch.

Now I'm Uncle Rex? Thought Rex to himself. *How the hell did this happen?*

"Uh, I guess?' said Rex, not really sure if this was good parenting or not.

"Please, please, please," Samantha begged.

"Fine, ya got a helmet?" asked Rex.

'I think Nina has one somewhere," said Samantha, getting up and racing towards Nina's bedroom.

Oh god, Eli is gonna come back from the grave and kill me if I somehow hurt his baby girl, thought Rex, realizing what could go wrong with teaching a teenage girl to ride a scoot.

Samantha returned some moments later with one of those Sons of Anarchy half helmets, which were popular about 20 years ago.

They wouldn't do jack shit if you came off your hawg doing 100 mph, but they certainly helped get around restrictive Helmet laws in states like California.

'Yeah, that works," said Rex. *Like she is going to get out of 1st gear today*, he thought to himself.

"Yay, I am so excited," Samantha declared.

"Hey. So, is there a huge parking lot anywhere around here? More importantly, a huge parking lot that no one uses on a Sunday?" asked Rex.

Samantha thought for a moment. There is an abandoned Costco about 2 towns over. Would that work?" she asked.

'Yeah, that should work," said Rex getting his ass out of the couch.

They left Nina's house, and Samantha locked it up on the way out. Rex started up his Harley, and Samantha stood in awe, watching it come to life. He let it idle for a minute, then swung his right leg over his machine as he had done a thousand times before. Once he was ready, he gestured for Samantha to get behind him.

She scrambled aboard and put her arms around him. He was a little taken back at first, but since there was nothing sexual going on between them, he shrugged and figured it was better to have her hold on safely than go over the back of his bike.

Rex headed North on the 77 Highway, and with a few wild hand gestures from Samantha, she led him to the town of Summer Haven. This town had seen better days. Whatever the source of income the town ever had was long gone. Logging? Rex assumed. Didn't matter now, seemed like a lot of residents had just packed up and walked out of their houses. *They could film a Zombie film here,* though, Rex, and they wouldn't need much in the way of Special Effects to mess the town up.

Samantha continued to guide him until they reached the site of the abandoned shopping complex. A huge car park, some form of monument to Western Consumerism of the 1990s or possibly the early 2000s. Probably in another 20 years, the car park would disappear, hidden forever more by nature. But for now, there was enough asphalt for Samantha to learn to ride.

He found a decent location in the car park with a lot of space between his bike and the nearest obstacle. Rex had been sent numerous videos over the years of people learning to ride and shooting straight into a fence or a parked car. It wasn't going to happen on his watch. Totally dumb.

He shut his bike down and nudged Samantha to get off. Once she was off, he swung his leg over and dismounted. He pulled off his helmet and gestured that she do the same.

Rex spent the next thirty minutes giving Samantha a rundown of the bike's controls. This is the clutch, this is the front brake, this is the rear brake. He tried to think back to when he learned to ride, but it had all come so naturally to him; besides, that was a long time and many, many beers ago.

Samantha seemed to be taking it all in, and it was a welcome relief to see a teenager whose head wasn't buried in a cell phone. Rex then explained the friction zone and its relationship to the clutch and changing gears. He then had her sit on the bike and did a quick test, asking her which control was the front brake, back brake, etc.

He could tell she was nervous, and Rex did his best to put her at ease on his Harley. At least her feet could touch the ground on both sides, which would give her some confidence and save the girl from dumping his bike.

He had Samantha put the bike in neutral and then turn on the ignition. He reassured her she would be okay. Then he asked her again to show him which one was the brake and which was the clutch. She got them right. He had Samantha squeeze in the clutch and put the scoot into first gear. Then he had her do friction zone drills for the next 5 minutes. Let the clutch out slowly, let the bike roll a couple of feet, squeeze the clutch back in again, and then repeat.

Once she had mastered that basic skill, he had her roll ahead very, very slowly. She screamed half in fear and half in delight as she rolled away doing all of 5 miles per hour. Rex made sure to keep pace with her and coached her all the way.

Within thirty minutes, he had her cruising the large abandoned parking lot, only in first gear, but he didn't want to push her so far on her first day. Eli would be proud of her skills. She was a natural. The apple doesn't fall far from the tree and all that. Who knows? Maybe she will be an award-winning bike builder in the years to come.

The sun was starting to go down on the horizon. Rex figured this was a good time to wrap it up. Samantha did a couple of figure-eights in the car park and then pulled up next to him.

"Who, I get it now," she said, jumping off Rex's Harley, elated.

'Get what?" he asked.

'Why are you guys so obsessed with your bikes? It's a feeling," she explained.

"Oh yeah, THAT." Riding had become so much of Rex's life that he had forgotten that original rush of endorphins you got on a bike versus driving in a car. 'Wait till you do 100 miles per hour for the first time."

"I can do that?' she asked incredulously.

"Yeah, one day, but guess what, kid? That day ain't today. You have to build up for that. You didn't even get out of first gear today," Rex explained.

"Oooh! When can we go again?" she asked excitedly.

"Ehh, sometime soon?" said Rex, more a question than a statement.

"Awesome, I can't wait," said Samantha.

'Anytime," Rex replied.

"Dammit," said Samantha.

"What now?' asked Rex.

"I gotta get my own bike!' Samantha explained, "How much do they cost?"

'Too much for the likes of you," Rex teased.

"Oh, come on!' groaned Samantha.

'Yeah, come on, indeed. We should head home now. Jump on," said Rex, nodding towards his passenger seat.

As soon as Rex got Samantha back to Nina's house, she was straight back on her phone and disappeared into her bedroom. Rex positioned himself on the couch, flicking through the TV stations to find something decent to watch, and then Clay and Nina returned home.

The two lovebirds came home at about 8.30 PM. Rex said his goodbyes and gave Clay a ride back to their motel. He wanted an early night since this was their last run to Vegas, and Rex wanted to be well-rested and on high alert for the ride back and forth.

He parked his bike in front of their motel room, and they spent the rest of the night flicking through the TV Channels and talking shit about the shows that were airing.

CHAPTER 33

Rex woke at 6 am. He wanted to give his bike the once over before their road trip to Vegas. He took a quick shower and brushed his teeth, reflecting that maybe it would have made more sense to shower on his return to Pine Hollow. Oh well, it's too late now.

He dressed, pulled on his heavy engineer boots, and went to check on his Hog. To his dismay, his rear tire was flat. He checked the tire over, finding a massive slash near the top of it. Damn, must have ridden over something sharp last night, giving Clay a ride back to their motel. Had it been a solo ride, he would have noticed it. Fuck, no time now to change the tire out, even if he had a spare in the motel room. He would have to face Cody and let him know that unless they could provide him with another bike or even a car, he was going to be much help to them today.

Frustrated, he went back inside to check on Clay. To his surprise, Clay was up and in the bathroom. Rex could hear the shower going. Okay, good. At least they could get down to the warehouse in time and figure out alternative plans with Cody.

Clay must have noticed the look of concern on Rex's face when he exited the bathroom.

'Everything okay, bro?" he asked.

"Nah, the Back tire is flat. Must have ridden over a piece of scrap metal on the way home last night," Rex replied.

"Oh shit, man, we don't even have a spare. What are ya gonna do?" asked Clay.

"I am just gonna have to go there and tell Cody my bike is out of commission. Maybe he can loan me a spare bike or a car for me to scout ahead, ya know? There's got to be some options." Rex suggested.

'What about Samantha's chopper?" asked Clay.

"Nah, what if I get chased again? We don't want her getting pulled over every 5 minutes, do we?" asked Rex.

'Shit yeah, I didn't even think of that," Clay replied. 'What about your bike though?"

"Maybe we can stop in Snowflake or Flagstaff and grab a new tire there?' Rex suggested. "Let's just get today's run done, and then we can figure that out."

"Yeah, sounds good," said Clay, pulling on his boots 'You about ready to go?"

"Yeah, bud, I'm just waiting on you," Rex replied. "You ready?"

"Yeah, let's go get Samanthas's bike back! Today IS the day!' Clay exclaimed.

"Indeed it is!" Rex smiled. "Let's get the fuck out of here."

Clay locked their motel room door as they left and then stopped to eye Rex's scoot.

"Ohh, that hurts the soul just to look at," said Clay.

'Tell me about it," Rex replied, shaking his head.

They made small talk as they walked down the street towards the warehouse.

"You know, it's kind of ironic, isn't it?' said Clay.

'What is?' asked Rex.

'Well, you lost access to your bike, and I will get mine back today," Clay explained.

'Oh shit, that's right, you get your Scoot AND your van back today! Stoked for you, bro," said Rex.

'Yeah, it's been too long, man. I'm getting with drawl symptoms here," said Clay

"I bet. Hey, maybe I can get Spike to bring up a spare tire and some wrenches from Phoenix! Thank you for reminding me," said Rex.

Rex dialed Spike's number, but it went straight to voice mail. It was still relatively early, so he texted Spike with his request for a new rear tire.

They quickly made it to the run-down warehouse. The "ice cream" van was there, but no sign of Cody. *No biggie, he must be inside,* thought Rex.

They hit the buzzer and waited. To both biker's surprise, Dan answered the door. Instead of inviting them inside, he stepped out of the warehouse and closed the door behind himself.

'Hey guys, a bit of bad news," Dan started to say

"Okay.." said Clay, cutting Dan off mid-flow.

"Cody can't make it today, so one of you want to drive?' he asked the pair.

"We can take it in turns," Rex suggested. "But what about the connect in Vegas?"

"I can call ahead and give them the change. They know both your faces, so it will be cool," Dan explained. "You pull up out front, go to the door, knock, and ask for Steve. Once he checks you off, he will tell the boys round back to let ya through, and they will load you up."

"Ok, no problem, we can take care of that for ya," said Rex. "Keys in the van?"

"Nah, I got 'em here," said Dan, rummaging through his pockets to find them. He pulled out a set of keys and clicked the lock/unlock button. Sure enough, the little van beeped away.

"Thanks," said Rex, taking the keys off Dan.

"Any questions?" asked Dan

Rex thought for a moment. 'Nah, I think we're good. I'll call ya if something comes up."

"Ok, well, safe travels," said Dan. "See ya when ya get back."

"You can bet on it," Clay retorted. "You taking the first shot at driving, brother?"

"Clay, I can drive to Flag, and we can switch there if ya want' said Rex. "I'm not fussy."

CHAPTER 34

R ex pulled out of the car park/loading bay and took a left on the side street that led them back to Main Street in Pine Hollow. He had no problem with driving cars; in fact, these days, most cars are almost too easy to drive. Back-up cameras and collision detection wing mirrors all made driving a vehicle easier. Soon, you would just tell your computer to drive you, and you could sit back and scroll through Instagram as your car dutifully did all the work. It wasn't like that riding his scoot. Your mind was going the entire time; any loss of focus could mean a fatal error. Your body almost became one with the bike to be a successful rider.

Very Zen-like or something. He could almost hear the old playground joke, "Confucius says the man who likes to ride a bike becomes the bike," or something like that. Cars were necessary, though, especially in the Tucson summers; crank that Air con up and stay cool as opposed to breathing in air so warm it taxed your lungs on your scoot. He couldn't wait to get his bike fixed and be back on 2 wheels as opposed to 4. Oh well, it was only for today. Spike and the guys would be up in Pine Hollow soon enough.

It was almost like Clay had read his mind.

'Wow, that worked out perfectly, didn't it?" asked Clay.

"Huh? What?" asked Rex, who was still deep in thought.

"Well, like you were going to have to tell Dan that you couldn't ride today, and then we found out Cody wasn't available. So you get to ride with me. I mean, perfect? Right?" Clay enthused.

"Oh yeah, yeah, definitely," Rex replied. It was perfect. It was also weird that Dan didn't ask where Rex's motorcycle was.

"How long to Flagstaff?" asked Rex. "I'm starving."

"Soon, buddy, soon," Rex replied, pulling onto Highway 77 and heading North.

They made it to "their" breakfast diner in Flagstaff. Now Rex was hungry, too. They ordered up and waited for their food to be delivered while cradling hot coffees.

"Hey, you remember the time we went to that house party in the Catalina Foothills?" asked Clay

"What? The one at that rich chick's place?" asked Rex.

'Yeah, that one!'" Clay replied, "That was a great night out."

"Haha, all the rich dudes hated us. The sons of doctors and lawyers. Always down to fight, but if you hurt them, Daddy is gonna sue yer ass," laughed Rex.

'Yeah, a lot of the girls loved us, and the guys hated us," said Clay

"Rich girls love a bad boy. Everyone knows that," said Rex.

"I think we all got laid that night," said Clay. "Man, they don't do house parties like that anymore, do they?"

"Nope, but remember, we almost had to fight our way out of there," said Rex

'Yeah, I think Eastside Rob banged one of their girlfriends; that was the final straw," Clay added.

"Ha ha, damn, that's right," laughed Rex 'He never gave a fuck did he?"

"Nope. Yeah, man, those dudes almost chased us all the way back to Tucson," said Clay.

"Yeah, we barely escaped," said Rex 'Those were the days, eh?"

'Yeah, these days, knowing our luck, we would probably get shot," said Clay

"Yeah, probably. Shit, do kids even do house parties these days?" Rex wondered.

"You know what, I don't know," said Clay.

"Yeah, me neither," laughed Rex. "All I know is I am glad we grew up when we did. You couldn't get away with half the stuff we did as kids cuz of smartphones."

"Yeah, that's true!" Clay replied, 'What amazes me is the number of kids who commit crimes, film it, and post it online. That's "exhibit A," in court right there."

'Self-incriminating – what a bunch of dumbasses," laughed Rex.

Finally, their food arrived, and with no mix-ups in their order, they both tucked it into their breakfasts.

They finished their food and coffee, and Rex went and paid. They were then ready to hit the road and continued their journey to Vegas. While Rex enjoyed shooting the shit with Clay and swapping stories about the old days, it bothered him his bike was out of commission. It was fine just yesterday. He knew how easily punctures can happen, but usually, he had some idea while riding that there was a problem, and he didn't get a hint of any of that last night. Especially significant damage to his rear tire like that.

At least the Phoenix boys were en route to Pine Hollow with Clay's van and scoot and a replacement tire for himself. Hopefully, the boys will stay in town for a few days and hang out before returning home.

The rest of their trip to Las Vegas was uneventful. As expected, traffic on the outskirts of Vegas has started to get busy, but there is no sign of cops or Feds. All good.

They found the suburban stash house without issue. Clay stayed in their van while Rex got out and approached the front door. The first thing he noticed walking up was the Ring camera mounted by the door. Whoever was approaching would be seen by anyone inside monitoring the screen. He rang the buzzer.

"Yes?" a voice asked.

"I am here to see Steve," Rex explained.

"Who sent you?" asked the voice.

"Dan," Rex replied.

'Who?" asked the voice.

"Dan, ahh, his usual guy is Cody, you know Cody," Rex stated.

"Oh! Cody, yeah, cool. Actually, someone did call about that earlier. You're gonna need to swing around the back, and my guys will take care of you out there. Do you know how to find the alley?' the voice asked.

"Yeah, we know the alley; thanks, we will be right there," said Rex, walking away. *Interesting,* he thought *They knew of Cody but not Dan. Dan must insulate himself to a level from these guys.*

He returned to the van, and they pulled out from the curb, heading up the block to the alleyway that ran parallel to the house.

The same sketchy tweaker dude opened the back gate for them to pull into the yard, then dutifully closed it again. Rex told Clay to stay in the van unless there was trouble, but he got out to open the back doors to load in. Before he had even managed to reach the van doors, the rear door of the stash house opened, and two dudes came out carrying those U-haul moving boxes. One of the guys who came from inside looked familiar to Rex, but the other did not. He wondered just exactly how many guys were in that house.

The guy that Rex had seen before nodded at Rex as he loaded up the van. So, maybe the guy recognized Rex as well? Who knew for sure? The two men loaded up the van and returned to the house for more boxes.

"Need help?" Rex asked the familiar-looking dude.

"Nah, we're good, only one more load to go," the man shouted over his shoulder as he fitted more U-haul boxes into the back of the Ice Cream van.

Another load? That didn't seem right. In fact, the way Rex figured it, this was significantly more product than the last 3 runs.

After the two dudes had finished filling the back of the van with boxes, they slammed the back doors and patted the vehicle with a "good to go" pat.

"Hey," Rex shouted to the talkative guy 'You sure this is the right order? Seems way more than usual."

The guy looked at Rex as if Rex had just taken a dump on their driveway.

"Yeah, your boss ordered more today. I guess business is booming. All good." without waiting for a reply from Rex, he turned, entered the back of the house, and slammed the door shut.

I guess the conversation is over, buddy? Thought Rex. *Nice chatting with ya, asshole.*

He nodded to Mister Janky, the looking dude on gate duty, and got back into the ice cream van. Tweaker dude was good at his job, as the moment Rex started backing up the van, the gate was wide open and ready for them to pull through. He turned to wave goodbye to the guy, but by the time he had looked around, the gate was shut again. No messing around here. Rex wondered if they ever got raided by rival gangs or if they had numerous stash houses around the city. That's what he would do. Have multiple houses and move them on random days. He assumed whoever was behind this operation did the same.

They took off down the alleyway.

"Doesn't this seem like a bigger shiPMent than normal?" asked Clay

'Yeah, he said. Dan upped his order," Rex replied. "I assume it's all paid for upfront or something?"

"I'm sure guys like that don't extend lines of credit," Clay said.

'Yeah, I am sure you are right," said Rex.

They cruised the surface streets of the Vegas suburbs, heading towards the Freeway south. Clay heard his phone go. He pulled his phone from his vest pocket and looked down. It was Spike from their Phoenix Chapter. Up ahead, he saw a 7-11 in a shopping plaza.

"Hey, I'm gonna take this," he said to Clay. Rex hated talking on the phone and driving at the same time. He felt by doing both, you sucked at both focusing on the road and what was said during a call. "I'm gonna pull over. Go grab me a fountain soda, would ya?" Rex nodded at the 7-11 in front of them.

By the time Clay had returned from inside the convenience store, Rex was done with his call.

Clay handed Rex an ice-cold fountain soda, and along with his own soda, Rex noticed that Clay had a giant family-sized bag of Funyuns, too.

Jumping back into the driver seat and putting his soda into the drinks holder, he turned to Clay.

"Funyuns, eh? I haven't had them since I was a kid," said Rex.

"Yeah, they're so good here, have some," Clay replied, pushing the giant-sized bag in Rex's direction.

Rex grabbed a handful as he put the van in reverse and pulled out of the shopping plaza.

"Damn, these are better than I remembered," Rex exclaimed

'Yeah, I told ya," smiled Clay. 'Who was that on the phone?"

"Spike from Phoenix, meeting up with us soon," Rex explained.

"Oh cool," Clay replied 'Hopefully, they can stay a couple of days and party with us."

'Yeah, that would be great," said Rex, spying the on-ramp for the Freeway south. "Let's get out of this town."

'Fine by me," said Clay.

Rex merged the van into southbound traffic as he slurped on his fountain soda.

"Hand me the Funyuns, bro," he asked Clay.

Clay shoved the bag in his direction. "Here ya go."

Rex grabbed another handful of the junk food and dumped them in his lap so he could nibble on them as he drove. "Thanks," he said to Clay, pushing the bag back in Clay's direction.

Soon enough, traffic was thinning out, and the drive got more relaxed. Only a handful of trucks and cars heading to Kingman or Phoenix rode ahead of them.

"Hey, we should do that, "Firing a 50-caliber rifle," thing with Spike and the guys," Clay suggested.

'Yeah, I definitely want to do that," said Rex 'You can drive a tank too, did ya see that?"

"Yeah, that looks good too," laughed Clay 'We could have done with a tank on some of the battles we found ourselves in over the years, eh?"

'You got that right!' said Rex, laughing at the idea of crushing their enemies' Harleys with a tank back in Tucson.

Clay spent the next 30 minutes messing about with his cell phone. Looking over while trying to drive, Rex figured he was texting with Nina. What happened to keep some mystery in your relationship? What was the old saying? "Give her the gift of missing you." Yeah, that sounds about right. Let her wonder where you are. Let her wonder what you are doing. Chicks love a bit of mystery. If you were an open book on everything, you lose that "mystery."

"Hey, why don't you leave that damn contraption alone?" Rex asked Clay.

"Aww, I'm just talking with Nina, bro," Clay shrugged.

"Well, you talk now. You won't have anything to talk about later," suggested Rex.

"Yeah, we always have something to talk about," Clay giggled.

"Damn, you two are like teenagers in love, bro. How old are you again?" he asked Clay.

"I'm 12," joked Clay

'Yeah, you got that right. You're 39 years old physically and mentally, age 12," joked Rex.

'Screw you," said Clay in a huff. He did one final text and put his phone away.

"Besides, you're meant to be a second set of eyes on the road to watch out for cops," Rex added.

"Fine," Clay replied.

Geez, it's like driving with a petulant 5-year-old girl, thought Rex.

"Thanks, man, just keep dem eyes peeled," said Rex.

"You got it, BOSS," said Clay. Rex couldn't tell if he was being a wise-ass or not.

They followed Highway US 93 as they wove their way south. After another 15 minutes, he could see the Gus's Jerky building in the distance. He needed to make a quick stop there. He looked over; Clay was fast asleep. *That lazy bastard* fumed Rex. *Oh well, let him sleep;* Rex had everything under control.

He reduced speed as they got closer and closer to Gus's Fresh Jerky. A quick 15-minute stop here, and then they would make their way straight to Pine Hollow. He flicked on the van's indicators and pulled into their car park. Quick stop, then back on the road.

Rex did what he had to do, then stepped into the Jerky store and picked up a couple of packets of their famous Cowboy jerky plus two bottles of soda before exiting the building and getting back into their van. With all the noise he was making, he was genuinely surprised that Clay had not woken up.

In fact, it wasn't until they hit the I-40 heading East that Clay woke up.

"Whoa, shit," he exclaimed.

"You okay, bro?" asked Rex.

'Yeah, I'm fine. I must have drifted off for a second there," Clay explained.

'Yeah, a second or two, I think," said Rex.

"What did I miss?" he asked.

"Hmm, just some trucks and some cactuses," Rex replied.

"Isn't it Cactii?" asked Clay

"What are you talking about?" asked Rex, trying to keep both eyes on the road.

"Isn't the plural of one cactus, Cactii, not Cactuses?" asked Clay.

"Dude, what do I look like? An English teacher?" said Rex.

Clay looked over at his buddy and eyed him up and down. "Yeah, a little bit. Yeah, you do."

"Fuck you, man!" laughed Rex. "I don't care what the official term for multiple cactus is, bro. I was simply making a point that you didn't miss much."

'Alright, alright, calm down broski," teased Clay

"FUCK.YOU," laughed Rex. 'I am calm."

The pair were having a good time traveling east across Arizona. Soon, they would be entering Hopi Country.

"Man, I love the Hopi Indians," said Clay

"Oh yeah?" asked Rex

"Yeah! We should do that Hopi reservation tour sometime," Clay suggested.

'Yeah, that could be cool," said Rex. "I would be down for that."

'Alrighty then. I'll see if Samantha and Nina wanna come with us, maybe this Sunday?" said Clay.

"Yeah, cool," said Rex 'Look into it and let me know."

"Will do," said Clay, picking up his phone and madly tapping away again.

Rex drove on.

"Damn," Clay exclaimed

"What's up?" asked Rex

'Well, it ain't cheap," said Clay

'What isn't cheap?' asked Rex

"The tour?" Clay replied.

'What tour? What are you talking about?" asked Rex.

'To tour a Hopi reservation, we are looking at about $340," said Clay

'Split 4 ways? That ain't bad," said Rex.

"Nah, bro. EACH," said Clay

"Oh damn," said Rex

"Yeah, exactly," said Clay

'Well, think about it. That's their spiritual land and shit; they probably need the money for upkeep and whatnot," Rex rationalized.

"Yeah, true," said Clay, feeling a bit dejected.

"You're gonna have to save up a couple of bucks now if ya still wanna go," teased Rex, still watching the road.

"I'll think of something," said Clay defiantly.

'Yeah, of course you will," Rex replied with a suitable level of snark.

Up ahead on the I-40 East, he could see the signs for Holbrook, which would be their exit.

Rex slowly started moving their van towards the exit lane. He was careful to signal for each lane change. Wait a moment, signal, and change again. He didn't need any stupid errors letting them get pulled over at this point. He had seen too many videos of criminals making minor traffic violations and getting busted.

He reduced his speed down to 45 mph as he took the exit towards Holbrook. In moments, they would be on the AZ-77 heading south and then home. Pine Hollow. The final run for scum bag Dan, and then they would have Samantha's Chopper back where it rightly belonged. He hadn't thought they would be able to get it back, but now it was happening. Rex realized that he had been stressed about getting Samantha her chopper ever since Clay had messed everything up. Deliver the shiPMent. Get the Chopper. Gift Samantha the Chopper. Fulfill Eli's dying request. Head home. Job done. They had done it.

They passed through the town of Snowflake, and Clay still had his nose buried in his cell phone. *Such a teenager* thought Rex, mentally shaking his head in disgust. There was a large Walmart truck ahead of them. *Fuck, you see, these guys all over the nation* thought Rex. *People need their low-priced products,* thought Rex. He kept a decent distance behind the big 18-wheeler. The last thing he needed now was to be clipped by the Long Haul truck with only miles to go before their destination.

He checked his rearview mirror. Two cars behind them, no rush. Heck, if they wanted to, there was nothing stopping either car from jumping in the fast lane and overtaking both him and the Walmart truck. He wasn't going to risk it.

"15 minutes," Rex announced.

"Until we get home?" asked Clay

"Yeah"

"Ok, cool, thanks," said Clay. Who started texting furiously again. Clearly telling Nina Rex figured.

Rex smiled to himself. Clay could be such a big kid at times.

The smile didn't last long. All of a sudden, the SUV that had been driving right behind them turned on police lights. WTF!!??

CHAPTER 35

Clay looked up in shock.

'Fuck bro, the cops," he exclaimed.

"Yeah! I can see that," said Rex 'Where the hell did they spring from?"

"I dunno, I never saw them," Clay said.

Yeah, cuz you were too busy texting, Rex thought to himself, "Dunno, bro."

'Were you speeding?" Clay asked

"No. Of course not," Rex replied.

'Gotta just be a routine check then, eh?" asked Clay.

'Yeah, I think so. Just stay calm, and we will be fine," Rex replied.

'Okay, okay," said Clay, not sounding very calm.

"Remember, don't give any more information than required. Don't overshare, and try not to be nervous," Rex advised.

"Okay, got it," said Clay

Rex found a safe spot to pull over and put the van in the park. He took a deep breath to steady his nerves.

The unmarked SUV pulled over behind them. Shutting down the cherries and berries as they did so.

The driver got out and approached their van on Clay's side. Rex nudged Clay to bring his window down.

'Afternoon officer," Rex greeted the uniformed cop.

'License and registration, please," asked the cop.

Rex handed the law enforcement officer his driver's license 'Here you go," he said.

"and registration?" asked the Cop.

'Ahh, this is our boss's van; let me check," Rex explained. "Clay, bud, can you check the glove box for me?"

Clay popped the glove box open and rummaged around. Pulling out a handful of papers.

'Tucson, eh? You're a long way from home," the Cop said, looking over Rex's license.

"Sir, can I see your license, too?' the cop asked Clay.

Clay stopped searching the papers. 'Why? I wasn't driving," he stated.

"Yes, I know that. I just like to know who I am talking to," said the cop 'Besides, you might have some warrants or something. Just need to check, okay?"

Clay looked over at Rex, almost like he was asking for permission. Rex nodded. "Go ahead"

Rex handed the cop his license. "Hmm, Tucson too, eh?"

"Born and raised," said Clay with a fake smile on his face. Maybe they would be able to get out of this after all.

"I am just gonna run your licenses; I'll be right back," the cop explained. The cop returned to his SUV.

"What do you think?" asked Clay

'We'll be fine, bro, just stay calm," Rex reassured Clay.

The cop returned. "Okay, here you go. There are no warrants," the cop remarked.

"Yes, sir. We're good boys," Clay said.

"So, what are you doing up in our neck of the woods?" The cop asked.

"Up here for work," Rex stated.

'No work in Tucson?" asked the cop.

"Just felt like a change," said Clay.

'Do you have that registration for me?" asked the cop.

"Yeah, I finally found it. Here you go," said Clay, passing the van's registration to the cop.

The cop spent a minute reviewing the paperwork before handing it back.

'Thanks," the cop said. Clay returned the paper to the glove box.

"Can you tell me why you pulled us over?" Rex asked the cop.

"Yeah, you were following that truck too closely," explained the cop. 'When you are trailing a big 18-wheeler like that, you have to leave yourself more of a safety gap."

Bullshit thought Rex. *There was plenty of room.*

"Ah, I see," he replied.

"So let me ask you. When was the last time either of you smoked weed?" said the cop.

"Not in years," said Clay

"I don't like weed," Rex replied.

'Smells like one of you was smoking in here recently," said the cop.

Clay sniffed the air. "I can't smell a thing."

While Clay was talking to the cop, Rex saw another unmarked vehicle pull up. *Reinforcements.*

The cop looked back at the second vehicle and nodded.

'Would you care if I searched the vehicle?" the cop asked Rex. Rex was calm, but he saw a look of fear on Clay's face. The cop, however, didn't seem to catch it.

'Yeah, I do mind," said Rex 'No reason to search us."

"Well, if you want to be difficult, we can be too. I can call for a K-9 unit and do a sniff test, or you can consent now and be on your way in 5 minutes," said the cop very calmly.

'No consent," Rex stated firmly.

The cop looked back and waved at his partner sitting in their SUV. The second cop got out and approached their van on Rex's side.

Here we go, thinking of Rex's *time to be bagged and tagged.*

'Sir, can you step out of the vehicle?" asked the 2nd cop of Rex.

The original cop pulled on the passenger side door handle. "Can you step out too?" he asked of Clay.

'What for? We haven't done anything," Clay protested.

"Just do it," sighed Rex. Over the years, he had seen cops charge his club brothers for "Resisting arrest" for simply verbally protesting, the irony being that would be the only charge they would get someone on. Very convenient for the cops.

They both stepped out.

"I'm just going to put these cuffs on for my safety," the cop with Rex explained to him. Over the other side of the van, he could hear the original cop saying the same thing to Rex.

They were both led back to the unmarked police SUV. Rex tried to get a closer look at their buddies in the 2nd vehicle but couldn't really see anything of note.

They were put in the back seat of the SUV, which had a holding cage installed. Rex hadn't been in the back of one of these for at least a decade now. As soon as he sat down, all the old (bad) memories came flooding back. He had sworn time and time again he would never let himself fall back to this again, yet here he was.

'Fuck," said Clay out loud. Rex kicked his leg with his boot. He knew damn well that these modern police cruises had cameras in the back seats. Even if they didn't find anything with their search, you said anything dumb in the back seat, well, guess what? You're gonna be charged with that.

Clay was sweating bullets. Rex watched as they tried to figure out how to unlock the rear doors of the 'Ice Cream" van.

The 2 new cops finally got out of their vehicle and walked towards their van. DEA was emblazoned on the back of both their coach jackets. *The big guns* thought Rex.

Clay looked over at Rex with a look of panic in his eyes. A look that said, "I'm not getting to be with Nina for the next 10 to 15 years."

Rex simply nodded at him with a sly smile.

By now, the cops had figured out how to pop the back of the van open. They were pulling out the U-haul boxes. Clay was nearly beside himself with fear now. They were never getting that Chopper back from Dan. He had fucked their lives and poor innocent Samantha's too.

The four cops started tearing through the U-haul boxes. Pulling out their contents and staring at them. Examining them. Rex sat calmly, and Clay looked on in horror.

One of the DEA guys walked back to their motor vehicle to retrieve something. Walked back past the SUV that Rex and Clay were locked up in with a plastic-type kit. *Test kit gotta be,* thought Rex to himself. *Here we go.*

The DEA agent took the kit to the front of the van. No doubt, they were setting up a little impromptu lab on the hood of their van. The original cop took some of the jars from a box he had opened to the front of their van. Not long now.

'We're fucked," said Clay out loud. Without looking down, Rex kicked his leg again. 'Why? We've done nothing wrong."

"Uh yeah," said Clay, not very convincingly. They sat and watched as the FED boys went back and forth, bringing the contents of opened boxes to the front of their van. Finally, after 15 minutes of this stupid charade, the two DEA guys walked back past Clay and Rex and got into their vehicle.

"They must be calling for backup," Clay stated.

"Nah, why would they need two of them to do that? Hopefully, they are leaving," said Rex.

"No chance," Clay replied, sweat dripping off his forehead.

While Rex couldn't hear what they were saying, he could see the two original traffic cops standing by the passenger side of the van arguing with each other. So heated. He wondered what had gotten their panties in such a bunch.

He smiled confidently to himself.

"They're probably arguing about who gets to beat us with their billy clubs first," said Clay.

'Yeah, probably," shrugged Rex.

'Really?' asked Clay.

"No, I was just a wise ass, bro. Just chill," snapped Rex, forever aware they were probably being filmed.

Just as he predicted, the DEA vehicle pulled away from them, leaving just the traffic cops.

"See," said Rex almost smugly.

'Dude...." was all Clay could manage to say.

Finally, the two cops stopped arguing. Now he could see they were discussing him and Clay. They kept talking and looking back at them. *They are wondering what to do now,* thought Rex.

The original cop approached Rex's side of the Cop car. His buddy approached Clay's side.

"Get out of the car," ordered Rex's cop, opening the locked bar door for him. Rex stepped out.

"Turn and face the vehicle," the cop instructed. Meanwhile, on the other side of the SUV, Clay's cop was doing the same thing.

Rex felt as the cop undid his steel cuffs. He shook his wrists to get the blood circulating again.

'You're free to go," said the cop. "Be more careful in tailgating next time."

"Yes, of course, officer," Rex remarked, barely able to hold back the glee in his voice. His partner did the same to Clay.

'Get those boxes cleaned up before you leave," shouted Clay's cop to Clay.

"Yeah, okay," Clay replied, shaking his head in defiance.

Rex and Clay loaded the ransacked U-haul boxes back into their minivan as quickly as they could.

"Dude, wtf? How?" hissed Clay to Rex as the two cops sat in their SUV glaring at them.

'Not now, in a few," Rex said quietly to the confused Clay.

Finally, they managed to load everything back in. They got back in the van, and Rex started backing it up. He put on the left turn indicator and waited for traffic to clear before pulling out into Southbound traffic again. He checked his rearview mirrors to ensure the traffic cops were not following them. They were not.

"What just fucking happened?' asked Clay. "Did you somehow do a "These are not the droids you are looking for," Jedi mind trick or something?"

Rex laughed. "Well, if you hold on a minute, I will explain."

Rex looked back to see if the traffic cops were still parked back there. They were.

CHAPTER 36

"Dude, okay, you have to tell me, how did you fool all those cops?' begged Clay as they headed south towards Pine Hollow.

"I didn't fool anyone," smiled Rex

'So how did we avoid arrest and imprisonment then?" he asked.

"Okay, let me backtrack. Getting that flat tire on my Harley this morning. Well, that was just weird. If I had hit something giving you a ride home, I reckon we would have noticed it," said Rex

"Could have been a slow leak or something?" Clay suggested.

"Yeah, it could have been, so I let it go. No way of knowing at that point," said Rex.

'Yeah, that's what I thought, too," said Clay.

"So yeah, we get to the warehouse, and Dan is there. Weird enough, but then he tells us no, Cody. That set the alarm bells ringing," Rex continued.

'I was just stoked I could ride with you and not him," said Clay.

"So again, 2 weird things. That's cause for concern but not necessarily an evil plot; you following me so far?" asked Rex.

"Yeah," Clay replied.

'So when we got to the stash house, they started loading us up with all those extra boxes of product. That's when I realized Dan was setting us up," said Rex

"That asshole! Wow, glad you figured it out," Clay replied. 'But what happened to all the products? I don't get it."

"Well, as we left the stash house, Spike called me; they were just about to hit the I-40 East and were asking where to meet," Rex continued.

"I remember that," said Clay.

"So I told them to hit the U haul in Kingman, buy up a ton of boxes, then hit a dollar store and buy a ton of cheap vitamins and crap," said Rex

'Oh, that's good," said Clay. "Wish I thought of that!"

"Thanks, dude. So yeah, I had them meet us at Gus's Jerky. You know the stop on US 93?" said Rex

"Of course, I love that place," said Clay.

'Well, you were sleeping, but we swapped out the boxes there, and they have them in your van," Rex explained.

"Oh shit! That's smart," said Clay.

'Since you didn't wake up, I figured it would be more believable if I didn't tell you," said Rex.

'Dude, I nearly had a heart attack sitting in the back of that cop car," said Clay

"Yeah, sorry. In hindsight, I should have warned ya. I was worried that you would say something incriminating in the back of their SUV. You know they have cameras back there to catch crims fucking up these days."

'Oh shit, I totally forgot about cameras back there," said Clay

'No worries, bro. I had your back. I am sure that's what they were doing when we left," said Rex.

'What's that?" asked Clay

"They were reviewing the tapes to see if we fucked up," said Rex

"Did we?" asked Clay

"Nah, I reckon if we did, they would have been all over us' said Rex.

'Why would Dan want to set us up?" asked Clay

'Well, my theory is this. He sets us up; it makes his brother look good. He assists in helping the DEA make arrests. Plus, he gets out of us getting Samantha's chopper back, and he gets to sell it or keep it for himself," said Rex

"That rat fuck," said Clay

"I get the feeling that corrupt cops have to make a few legit busts or at least assist in making busts to keep the heat off themselves," Rex elaborated.

'Yeah, I reckon you are right,' Clay replied.

Rex took the exit for Pine Hollow off the 77 freeway.

"What are we gonna do about Dan?" asked Clay

"We have to make a quick stop at the motel," smiled Rex.

"Oh, the boys are there? Yeah?" asked Clay

"Yeah, we can do a quick switcheroo back at the motel," said Rex.

They pulled into the motel carpark, and Clay's van and Harley parked two rooms down from their room. Rex pulled their minivan in right next to Clay's van. He then grabbed his phone and texted Spike. Moments later, Spike and 2 more of the Phoenix chapter of the Steel Reapers appeared from a motel room.

"What's up, sleeping beauty?" asked Spike of Clay.

Clay laughed. "Oh, man, am I glad to see you." he gave Spike a big bear hug.

Spike introduced the two other guys, Keith and Diesel. Neither Rex nor Clay had met either before.

Spike and Rex had a quick brainstorming session about Dan's product, and then, with the help of Keith and Diesel, they quickly loaded up the "Ice Cream" minivan with U-haul boxes. Rex and Clay said their goodbyes and headed down Main Street toward the warehouse.

Rex pulled the van close to the loading dock, leaving the van running, but in the park, he got out and hit the buzzer on the front door. Dan didn't show any shock on his face, but Rex could tell the guy was visibly nervous. However, he is doing his best to try and hide it.

"Hey man, good to see you," smiled Rex

"Uh, yeah, you too," said Dan. "Everything goes okay?" Dan looked around the car park as if expecting a SWAT team to come out of the shadows or something.

"Yeah, great, we're gonna unload now," smiled Rex. "Open up the loading bay, would ya?"

"Uh yeah, um sure," said Dan. Disappearing back into the warehouse.

As the steel gates automatically went up, Rex returned to the van and, with Clay's help, carefully unloaded all the boxes to the dock. Once they were all out of the van. They quickly grabbed the boxes, loading most of them straight onto the shelving that Rex had seen Dan's goons do in the past. He deliberately left a few of the boxes out in the parking area for the warehouse.

Within minutes, they successfully emptied the van and put all the boxes away. Dan hovered about nervously in his office.

"Okay, we are all done," Rex declared. 'I guess we should get going now."

Dan came out of his office like a bat out of hell.

"Hold on a minute. Just let me check the merchandise," said Dan.

"I figured you might want to," said Rex 'I left a few boxes out for you."

"I saw those!" said Dan, choosing to ignore them and grab random boxes from the shelves. Clay watched him like a hawk.

Clay looked over at Rex as Dan pulled a box cutter from the packing table and started to cut boxes open. Rex gave Clay a very subtle nod.

Dan grabbed a bunch of pills and baggies from various boxes and laid them out on the packing table.

'Let me just go grab a test kit," he said, returning to his office.

CHAPTER 37

Dan returned and pulled samples from various boxes, pills, and powders lying across the packing table. Rex and Clay stood silently, watching him as he ran a battery of tests on his products. Moments later, the law enforcement standard drug tests were turning blue and or purple depending on the drugs he was testing. Everything was kosher.

'Wow, pure stuff," Dan declared.

"What were you expecting? Fake products? Has your connects stiffed you before?" Rex asked.

'No, no. But, ahh, it pays to check on them every now and then," Dan stammered.

'Ah, smart," said Rex with a smug look on his face.

"So, are we good to go now?" asked Clay.

'What? Uh, yeah, sure!" Dan replied.

Rex and Clay turned to leave. They got halfway to the door before Rex stopped and turned back.

"Actually, we forgot something," said Rex

"What's that?" asked Dan, checking the packing table 'Your cell phone?"

"No, our chopper!" Rex smiled.

'Oh, uh yeah, that. Totally forgot," said Dan. "Hey, would you consider a couple more runs for me? I mean, you have done such a great job, you two; I would love to give you more work."

Rex walked right up to Dan. "Naw, we're good. A deal, a deal, right? We shook on this. I took you as a man of your word, Dan."

"Yes, yes, of course. Let me go find the keys," Dan stammered. Dan scurried into his office and started pulling open his desk drawers. He returned with a set of keys.

"Ah, here you go," he said, handing them over to Rex.

"Thanks, Dan; it was a pleasure doing business with you." Rex smiled, handing the keys to Clay. Clay went off to find Eli's prize bike.

"Well, it's going to be a shame to see you go," said Dan to Rex.

'Listen, Dan. I tell you what. It's been, uh, interesting working with you. Just to show you that I have no hard feelings, I would love to take you out for a steak dinner tonight. There's a killer place in Flagstaff," Rex suggested.

'Dinner? With you? Uh, I mean, with you guys?" Dan stammered again.

"Sure, as a token of our appreciation," Rex smiled again.

'Um, sorry, I promised my brother Calvin I would hang out with him tonight," Dan explained.

"Well! Let's bring him along too," smiled Rex. 'The more the merrier, eh?"

"Uhhhh, Let me call him, I guess," said Dan 'He's probably busy, though."

'Well, if he was going to hang with you, he can't be THAT busy," said Rex. "Go ahead and call him; I'll wait."

Dan called Calvin as Rex stood watching. 'Yeah, them. Yeah, Steakhouse. Yeah, I know, I know," Dan said

"It's called Black Bart's Steakhouse," said Rex

"It's called Black Barts," Dan explained to his brother.

"Oh, you've been there before? Any good?" asked Dan.

"Ok, 7 PM. Yeah, sure," Dan hung up the phone.

"Well?" asked Rex. "All good?"

'Yeah, I guess we are going for steaks," said Dan

'Ok, cool. Let Clay and I take OUR chopper back to the motel and meet you back here around 630PM, eh?" Rex suggested.

"Ok, cool, I can fit everyone in my SUV," said Dan.

"Alrighty then, see you in 30," said Rex. 'Clay, you ready?"

"Yeah, all good here," Clay shouted from the front doorway. He had the chopper in his hands, rolling it outside.

Clay rode Samantha's soon-to-be chopper back up towards the hotel with Rex in the passenger seat. Nuts to butts.

"You wanna hit the bar tonight?" asked Clay when they got back to their motel.

"Nah, we're going for steaks in Flagstaff," said Rex

"What? With the Phoenix boys? Oh, cool," Clay replied.

"Nah, they got stuff to do tonight," Rex explained.

"Oh, okay. With Nina and Samantha then?" asked Clay

'Nah, with Dan and his brother," Rex smiled.

"Are you fucking kidding me?' said Clay 'They tried to set us up, and you want to reward them with steaks?'

"Hey, look, they tried, and they failed. We won. Buying them dinner is a mind fuck. It's like we are saying, 'We know what you tried to do, and we don't care," It's a flex or whatever the kids say these days," Rex explained.

"Damn dude, I dunno about this," said Clay shaking his head.

'Trust me, it's fine," said Rex. "Just follow my lead on this. I know what I am doing."

'if you say so, bro," said Clay, shaking his head.

"Hey, let's roll Samantha's scoot inside," said Rex 'I don't want to take any chances."

"Ok, bro," said Clay

'Then let's head straight back down to the warehouse, alright?'

"Yeah, cool," Clay replied.

Before long, they were riding in Dan's SUV on their way to pick up Calvin at his property on the edge of town. Clay sat in the front, and Dan and Rex sat in the back seat. Rex made a mental note of the street address and sent a quick text just as Calvin got into the back seat.

Calvin looked Rex up and down before sitting down next to him.

"Good to see you again," said Rex

"Oh, you guys met before?" asked Dan

"Yeah, it always pays to support your local sheriff," said Rex

"Damn straight," said Calvin.

Dinner was great. They all got prime rib, but Calvin wanted filet mignon. Rex made sure to keep the drinks flowing all night.

They told stories about their days growing up in Tucson and soon had both Dan and Calvin in stitches with tall tales about bar fights and shady ladies.

Rex paid the significant bill, and they all filed out to the car park to get into Dan's SUV. Just before leaving, Rex had to take a phone call. He made his excuses and told the guys to wait a moment while he dealt with the call. He walked to the other side of the car park and returned soon after.

'Everything okay?" asked Dan when Rex returned.

"Yeah, just my boss in Tucson asking when I will be coming back to work," said Rex

'OH yeah, and what did you tell him?' asked Calvin.

"Eh, I figure a couple more days and we will be heading back," Rex replied.

'Oh, be a shame to see you boys go," said Calvin

'Yeah, I know, but duty calls, ya know?" said Rex.

'Yeah, duty calls,' Clay repeated.

Dan dropped the two bikers off at their hotel, thanking them for dinner. After the brothers pulled out and undoubtedly headed back to their respective homes, Clay turned to Rex and asked.

'Ya wanna tell me what that was all about?"

"All in good time, my friend, all in good time." Rex smiled at his old buddy.

CHAPTER 38

Other than repairing his damaged tire, the rest of the week was fairly uneventful for Rex and Clay. On Thursday evening, Spike and the Phoenix boys hit the Dead Crow Saloon with the Tucson boys. Of course, the beers flowed, as did the Whiskey shots. Rex drank so much that he felt like he was blind. *That's probably where the saying "Blind Drunk" came from,* he thought to himself before passing out back at the motel that night.

The next day, he woke with a steaming hangover. He lay there quietly in his bed until he heard Clay stirring.

"Yo Clay, how ya feeling?" Rex asked his club brother.

"I'm feeling like I will never drink again," Clay groaned. "You?"

"Yeah... pretty much the same. How are we still alive after all the shit we do to ourselves?" Rex asked.

'We're medical miracles, brother," said Clay. "I gotta get some coffee. Shall we hit the diner in a second?"

"Yeah, definitely, bro. Hopefully, some greasy bacon and home fries will mop up all the booze in my system, " Rex replied.

"Ok, cool, let me piss and freshen up, and I'll be ready," Clay replied, slipping out of bed and hitting the bathroom.

20 minutes later, they were both out the door and walking down the main street to "their" diner.

'Don't you think we should have woken Spike and the boys?' asked Clay

"Nah, they know where to find us. Let 'em sleep it off," said Rex.

As they walked down the street, there seemed to be some electricity in the air. Something had happened in town. Everyone seemed to be talking in furtive whispers. Rex felt it right away. He wondered if Clay did, too.

As they were waiting to be seated at the diner, Rex heard someone calling his name. He looked to the back of the restaurant and saw Spike and the boys waving them over. They had taken over the big booth right next to the kitchen.

"Hey, it's the Phoenix boys; let's go," said Rex, gesturing to the back of the joint.

Clay followed Rex towards their club brothers.

"How ya feeling, ladies?" asked Diesel.

'Fuck you," laughed Rex 'Like total shit. You?"

"Pretty much the same," laughed Diesel. "Some coffee and good food will sort you out. Grab a seat."

"Thanks," said Clay, squeezing in.

'So you boys heard the news yet?' asked Spike with a huge shit-eating grin on his face.

'What news?" asked Clay.

'The big news is all over town," said Keith with a sly smile on his face.

'I KNEW there was something going on today!' said Clay. "I could just feel it."

"So don't leave the poor guy in suspense," Rex laughed. "Just tell him already!"

"Tell me what?" asked Clay.

'Well.." said Spike, barely containing his amusement. 'The crooked sheriff of this town and his brother both got busted yesterday with half a million in drugs by the DEA."

"No way' said Clay 'That's amazing."

"Yeah, good riddance to both those scumbags," Rex added.

"Wait a sec.." said Clay, looking at everyone in the booth 'Did you guys have something to do with this?"

'Whaaaaaa? Us?" Spike said with mock indignation, "Clay brother, you know the club has strict by-laws about talking to law enforcement."

"Oh, yeah, I know. I was just wondering cuz..." Clay replied.

Spike Keith and Diesel could barely contain their laughter now.

'Well, it's not to say maybe, someone's wife might have had a word to someone at the DEA that two douchebags had tons of product hidden away at their homes," Keith smiled.

"Oh wait, so..." said Clay. Rex could almost see the gears whirring away in his brain, trying to put the whole thing together. 'Okay, I'm confused. How?"

Rex turned to his buddy. "Well, when we made the delivery to Dan's warehouse. We kept half their product and gave them half product and half cheap vitamins, etc."

"Oh, we did?" asked Clay

"Then, when you and I took Dan and Calvin to dinner, Spike and the boys planted everything in their homes," Rex explained. 'Then

Keith's wife reached out to her sister, who is married to a DEA agent, and gave him a friendly tip about a Northern Arizona mountain town drug ring."

'No shit," swore Clay.

"Yeah, apparently, law enforcement had been after the brothers for years, but they were just too slippery," said Rex. "Justice finally caught up with them."

"So, that's why you were so kind buying them dinner," said Clay.

"Pretty much," laughed Rex 'Fuck those guys."

The Phoenix boys raised their coffee cups to toast the demise of the two brothers. Clay and Rex joined them.

CHAPTER 39

After breakfast, they started making plans to head back home and ride back with the Phoenix boys. Spend a night with them partying at their clubhouse, and then go home to Tucson. Rex was surprised his boss had let him keep his job after taking so much time off.

'So this Sunday, Nina has invited us all over for lunch at her place," Clay announced.

"Nina? She's the pretty blonde bartender at the dive bar, yeah?' asked Spike.

'That would be the one," Rex smiled. "Ol Clay is practically married to her now."

"Is that right?" asked Diesel. "You lucky bastard," he teased.

"Luck? No brother, all skill," Clay replied.

"Skill? You?" questioned Rex 'She could be lying naked on the bed, and you would be asking me, 'Do you think she likes me?" What's your level of skill with the lady's brother."

"Shut up," Clay replied. The Phoenix boys laughed.

"So, do we have to bring anything for Sunday lunch?" asked Keith.

"Eh, you can just bring some wine or beers, bro. She's a great cook. Do you some good to have some home cooking for a change?" Clay replied.

"So what about Eli's chopper?" asked Spike.

'Yeah, we are going to give it to his daughter Sunday after lunch. I can ride back with one of you guys and fetch it after we have eaten," Rex explained.

"I'll do it," Clay volunteered.

"Of course you will," teased Spike. "Anything to curry brownie points with Nina, ya simp."

"F.U.," Clay replied, giving Spike the finger.

'What plans have we got for the rest of the day?" Diesel asked everyone.

"I'm going back to bed," said Clay.

"We were thinking about checking out Flagstaff," Spike commented. "Clay, any chance we can borrow the van?"

"Yeah, any time," Clay replied, fishing for his keys out of his pocket.

"I know some spots in Flag," said Rex 'I can be your tour guide."

"That would be awesome," said Keith.

"Well, let's make a move to get out of here," said Spike. "Who's turn is it to pay?"

'I think it's Clay's," said Diesel. "We fixed his van and scoot, so yeah, definitely his."

'Fine, I'll pay," groaned Clay 'I already paid you boys for the work done, by the way."

"Yeah, I know," laughed Spike, "But it's still fun to bust your balls."

"Fuckers," swore Clay as he got up to pay at the register.

CHAPTER 40

Saturday night, the boys hit the Dead Crow Saloon for a few drinks. Sunday morning, Rex awoke with surprise, surprise, another hangover. He showered and dressed and then walked down to Spike, Keith, and Diesel's motel room to wake them up.

By the time he returned, Clay was in the bathroom, and he could hear the shower going on. *Good, that lazy bastard got up without being woken up for a change,* thought Rex.

The Phoenix boy's room smelled like stale beer and farts. After Spike let him in, Rex went to the window and pulled it open to let some fresh air in.

"What the fuck?' groaned Diesel 'Let me sleep."

'Time to get up, ya lazy bastard," laughed Rex 'We got lunch with Nina and Eli's daughter today."

"Already? Isn't it like 7 am?" asked Diesel.

"Nah, it's 11.30 am, you fucker," said Rex 'Wakey, wakey hand off, snakey."

Rex could hear Keith laughing under his covers.

"You too, Keith, chop chop," said Rex. Finally, Keith jumped out of bed and raced to the bathroom in his boxers. That was good enough for Rex 'Alrighty then. You boys have got 30 minutes."

'You sure it's not 7 am?" groaned Diesel.

"I wish it was," said Clay. "Jump in the shower when Keith comes out. Trust me, you will feel a lot better."

"Yeah, okay, Dad," said Diesel, rolling over in his bed.

"I'll make sure they're ready," said Spike. "Leave 'em to me."

"Thanks, Prez," said Rex, turning and leaving the room. *Hopefully, it would air out before the poor maid had to clean it,* thought Rex as he headed back to his room. He wanted to look over Samantha's chopper one more time before they gifted it to her today.

CHAPTER 41

Sure enough, 30 minutes later, all the Phoenix boys were up and ready for the ride over to Nina and Samantha's place. Rex rode his scoot, and Clay took the rest of them in his van. Despite Dan and Calvin being held without bail and awaiting trial, Rex made the decision to keep Eli's chopper for Samantha safely locked up in their motel room until he returned after lunch to collect it. He wasn't taking any chances with it getting stolen or damaged in the few short hours he would be away.

Nina greeted them at the door when they arrived. She dragged Samantha out of her room to get to know the Phoenix boys so she could get back into the kitchen and finish prepping lunch. Samantha bought them all beers from the kitchen and learned a little bit about Spike, Keith, and Diesel as they made small talk, waiting for food.

"Damn, woman, that smells great. How long until we can eat?" Clay shouted from the living room to Nina.

'About 5 minutes for the boys," Nina shouted back. "But since you were so rude, shouting instead of coming and asking me, you will have to wait another 30 minutes."

"Damn," laughed Spike 'That will teach ya," Diesel and Keith joined in with the laughter.

"Samantha, honey, come and help set the table," Nina shouted from the kitchen.

Samantha checked to make sure none of them needed another beer, then made her excuses to go help Nina set the table for lunch.

Finally, the boys were summoned to eat. Nina had Clay sit at the head of the table with her on his right and Rex on his left. Samantha sat at the opposite end from Clay, and the Phoenix boys squeezed in next to Rex and Nina on opposite sides.

Nina made them a huge plate of spaghetti with homemade meatballs and garlic bread. She offered them all a glass of red wine to go with their food. To which Spike and Diesel happily accepted. Samantha begged for a glass, too, but Nina refused her. Settling on a soda, she raised her glass to the table.

"Here is to new friends and old," she said 'I sure wish my dad was here to see this."

'Cheers," everyone replied

"I wish he were here too," said Rex 'He was a good man."

"Yes, indeed," Clay added.

'Damn, this is good, good, good," Spike declared with a mouthful of spaghetti and meatballs.

"Aww, thanks, hon," said Nina. "All home-cooked."

"See, I told ya." Clay smiled like a proud father.

By the time they had finished eating, everyone was pretty much stuffed with food.

"Damn, I wish I had worn sweatpants," said Keith. "You're a great cook, Nina."

"Thanks," said Nina. "Anyone want coffee?"

"No thanks, but I'll take another beer if you've got one," asked Spike.

"Sam honey, can you grab him another beer, please?" asked Nina

'Anyone else needs another beer?" Samantha asked, getting up and heading to the fridge.

"I'll take one," said Keith

"Me too," said Clay

"Me three," said Rex

"I'll stick to the wine," said Diesel.

Samantha handed beers to Rex and Clay and had them pass them down to the others.

Nina sent everyone back out to the living room so she and Samantha could clean up.

After a couple of sips of his beer, Rex put his bottle down and looked over at Clay.

"You ready?" he asked.

'For what?" Clay replied.

'For the thing! You know!' said Rex

'Ohhhhh, the "thing." yeah, duh," said Clay. "Now?"

"Yeah, now, before we get too sozzled," said Rex.

"Ok, let me kill this beer," said Clay, chugging the rest of his bottle.

'We will be back, gentlemen," said Rex 'Don't go away."

Rex gave Clay a ride on the back of his Harley to the motel. Once there, they parked up, and Rex held the motel room door open. Clay went in to retrieve the award-winning Chopper.

'Just take it nice and slow, bro," said Rex 'We don't want to dump the bike now, after all this."

"Yeah, yeah, I'm doing my best," Clay replied, using all of his brain power to focus on getting the scoot out of the narrow motel room door.

'Once the bike was out in the daylight, Clay put the kickstand down.

Rex looked over the bike like a high-end jeweler, looking for any blemishes or smudges on the prized Chopper.

He went back into the motel room and rummaged through his tool roll, eventually finding a microfiber cloth so he could give the bike a quick wipe-down before they delivered it to Samantha.

'I wanna do this, right ya know?" said Rex. "For both Samantha and for Eli."

'Yeah, I get it," said Clay, thinking about Eli and his legacy.

Rex spent about 5 minutes wiping the bike down and getting rid of any dirt and grime that had accumulated since it had been sitting in Dan's old warehouse. Finally satisfied, he tossed the rag back into the room and pulled their door shut.

"Ok, you good to ride this?' he asked Clay.

"Yeah, yeah, all good here," said Clay

"Needless to say, if you dump the bike, I'll drop kick ya all the way back to Tucson," threatened Rex.

"Well, I had better ride carefully then," joked Clay, mounting up the glorious bike.

The pair took their time and cruised at the slow rate of 30mph all the way back to Nina's place. When they returned, they found Nina and Samantha talking to the Phoenix guys in the living room.

Everyone stopped talking and looked up as they walked in.

"Where have you two been?' asked Samantha.

"Oh, we had to head back to the motel to collect something," Rex said, trying to contain his excitement.

'A present for me?" teased Samantha.

"Hmm," Rex replied. "To receive a present, you have to be well-behaved. By all accounts, that disqualifies YOU from ever getting a present."

"Aww, meanie, I hate you," laughed Samantha.

Everyone laughed.

"So, is now a good time?" asked Clay.

'Sure, why not?" Rex replied. "Nina wanna cover her eyes?"

"Sure, c'mon, kiddo, a big surprise awaits you," said Nina to Samantha.

"What? Are you serious?" asked Samantha 'You got me a puppy?"

"Yeah... kinda," Rex smiled.

Nina got up off the couch and stood behind Nina 'Ready?" she asked.

"Ugh, I guess," Samantha replied.

"C'mon guys," said Nina to Spike, Diesel and Keith. "This way."

Everyone got up and followed them out to the front yard.

Nina positioned Samantha in front of Eli's chopper.

"You ready?" she asked Samantha.

"I guess," she replied 'I don't hear a puppy."

Rex got out his phone and stood across the other side of the bike, facing everyone.

'I'm ready," said Rex with his cell phone camera trained on Samantha and Nina.

'Ta da," said Nina, removing her hands from Samantha's face so she could see the stunning motorcycle.

"Whoa! Nice bike!" said Samantha. "Who's is that?"

'YOURS!" Rex and Clay shouted in unison.

'What? Mine? No way! How?" asked Samantha, fighting back tears.

"Your father," said Rex.

'What??" asked Samantha.

"It was your father's dying wish to give you this bike," Rex explained.

Samantha was crying. "OH MY GOD, this is the best gift ever," she sobbed.

Nina comforted her as she let out tears of joy.

"You guys are the best. Thank you. Thank you. Thank you," she sobbed.

'It was the least we could do," said Clay 'Your dad was a great man."

"Yes, he was," Spike added.

'Well? You take it for a test ride?' asked Diesel.

"Ohh, can I?" asked Samantha, looking over at Rex.

"Sure, but go grab a helmet and put on some over-the-ankle boots," said Rex 'My gloves will be a bit big for you, but you can use them until you get your own."

Samantha raced into the house to fetch her helmet and some Doc Martin boots.

Yo, she gonna be okay doing this?" Spike asked.

"Yeah, she's a natural," Rex explained 'I'm only going to let her ride down the block and back and no faster than first gear."

"Okay, bro, as long as you are confident," Spike replied.

"I am. Well... yeah...sort of.." Rex replied.

Samantha returned with her riding gear. Rex pulled out his riding gloves from his back pocket and handed them to her.

'Here ya go, kiddo," he said

"Thanks," she replied, snatching them from Rex.

"Now you remember your training, right?

SLLLLOOOOOWWWWWLLLLLYYY release the throttle, and don't change out of first gear! At least not until you get the feel of her."

"Yeah, yeah," said Samantha, brushing away Rex's concerns. Everyone gathered around as Samantha pulled on her helmet and Rex's gloves.

To Rex's surprise, she started the Chopper right away and didn't dump the clutch. Soon, she was riding up and down the street like a pro.

"Like father – like daughter, eh?" said Spike.

"Apple doesn't fall from the tree, right?" Clay added.

'You're a natural!" Rex shouted as Samantha brought the chopper back to Nina's front yard.

'Really?" asked Samantha, pulling off her helmet.

'Yeah, for sure," everyone pretty much answered in unison.

"Must be in your blood," said Keith.

Samantha was grinning from ear to ear. "When can I go for longer rides?' she asked.

"I'll take you sometime this week," said Clay

Weird thought, Rex. *Did he forget that we are leaving for Phoenix on Monday?*

Everyone congratulated Samantha on her first ride and headed back inside for more beers. As they were heading in, Clay tapped Rex on the shoulder.

'Hey, I need a quick word," said Clay

'Sure, buddy, everything okay?" asked Rex.

'Yeah, all good. There's something I need to tell you," Clay explained.

Rex took a breath. *This didn't sound good. Oh boy, here it comes.*

"Yeah?"

"Yeah. Things between Nina and me have been going great," Clay started.

"Okay," Rex replied.

'So yeah, I ain't got much going on down in Tucson right now," Clay continued.

'Yeah, well, that's your home. You were born and raised there," Rex pointed out.

"Well, I guess what I am trying to say is that I think I might stay here," said Clay.

"Dude, motel living soon gets costly; you don't even have a job," said Rex.

Spike came outside to see what was holding up Clay and Rex.

'Everything okay, boys?" asked Spike.

"Yeah, all good," said Clay.

"Actually, he is telling me he's gonna stay in Pine Hollow," said Rex.

'Oh, that's cool. Move in with your old lady, eh?' asked Spike.

"Yeah, with Nina. Yeah," Clay replied.

'Smart man, she's a great cook," said Spike.

"Yeah, she is."

"I was just telling him he doesn't even have a job right now," said Rex.

"Actually, I was thinking of starting a motorcycle shop," Clay explained.

"Dude, you don't have any money," Rex pointed out.

"I'll figure it out," said Clay with determination.

'Actually, about that," said Spike. "We, eh, might have some extra cash we could invest, make it a club-owned shop."

"Let me guess where you got that cash," said Rex. "Maybe at Dan's place?"

"Ummm. Let's just say we somehow acquired it," said Spike with a big grin on his face.

"I see' said Rex.

'Wait, I'm confused. You got it from Dan or nah?" asked Clay.

"Of course he did," said Rex, shaking his head.

"So let me ask you a question," said Spike. "You still gonna give us a lift back to Phoenix in your van tomorrow?'

'Yeah, sure. I am gonna have to go back to Tucson to pick up my stuff anyways," said Clay.

'Okay, cool, much appreciated," said Spike. 'Hey, I gotta go back inside and join the boys."

Spike turned and walked back into Nina's home.

Rex's mind was reeling. For as long as he could remember, Clay and he had been side by side through good times and bad. It was going to be a massive re-adjustment to deal with life without him.

As if he could read Rex's mind, Clay asked him, "You cool, bro?"

"Yeah, yeah, just trying to process everything," said Rex. "You're gonna be missed."

'I hear ya man. But I got a good thing going here," said Clay.

'Yeah bro, trust me, I get it,' said Rex

"Look, Nina and I can still come down to Tucson to visit, and you know damn well you are always welcome here," said Clay. "'Shit, you could come up every other weekend, and we could ride down and see you too."

'That's true," said Rex.

'Besides, wouldn't you rather beat the Tucson summers?" said Clay 'Got to be at least 20 degrees cooler up here in the summer than home, ya know?"

"Well, in that case, ya better have a spare room ready for me," joked Rex.

'We will," said Clay.

'Awesome," said Rex 'I guess we had better join the others."

"Yeah, cool. Let's head in," said Clay

CHAPTER 42

M onday morning, Rex and Clay checked out of the motel. Clay rode his bike back to Nina's house with Spike following in his van and Rex on his scoot.

After storing his Harley safely in Nina's garage, he jumped into the van with the Phoenix boys.

The plan was to ride to Phoenix today. Have a night with the Phoenix chapter, and then continue on to Tucson Tuesday morning.

Rex leads the ride back south on the Az-77 highway. He reflected on their journey to Northern Arizona and the end of an era. Eli had passed. Cody was moving to Pine Hollow. They were parting ways after 30 years of friendship.

It was the end of the chapter and the start of a new one. They had come; they had achieved what they had set out to do. Grant the dying wish of their friend Eli. They had helped his daughter, and they cleared the small town of its criminal element. Not bad going. He was content in the knowledge he had done right by his brothers, and that was good enough for him. At least for now. Who knew what the next chapter of his life had in store for him? Only time will tell.

Their night in Phoenix was a blast, as it always was when they hung out with their club brothers. A club member called Dave, newly divorced, let them park at his 3-car garage and sleep there too.

They started off at a high-end Mexican restaurant, and of course, the margaritas were flowing like fine wine. After that, they ended up bar hopping until closing time.

Rex had no idea how they got back to Dave's house. For that matter, neither did Dave or Clay the next morning when he asked them. How do 3 different people remember the night in 3 different ways? Rex thought they got a Waymo, one of those self-driving Ubers, whereas Clay said they got caught in an Uber, and Dave insisted that one of the club guys drove them home. Somewhere, someone knew, but it wasn't any of them. One of life's mysteries.

They said their goodbyes to Dave and thanked him for his hospitality. Rex led the way as Clay drove his van out of the city South towards Tucson.

It was early afternoon by the time they got back on the road to Tucson. Rex was grateful that rush hour traffic out of the city hadn't started yet. He was in no shape to deal with heavy traffic and his hangover at the same time. What was the old saying? Never fight a war on two fronts?

Despite having two nights to sleep on it, Rex still had not adjusted to the idea of losing Clay. It would take time, but he would be fine. Before everyone got too drunk, Spike had hashed out a rough plan for the Steel Reapers motorcycle shop in Pine Hollow. Considering there was no bike shop in any of the surrounding towns, it sounded like they actually had a chance of making it work. Both Rex and Clay had been wrenching on their bikes since their teenage years and could pretty much fix any problem that Clay might encounter. Who knows, maybe it would work out for Clay up there.

As with most things in life, time will tell.

Rex rode on down the well-traveled I-10 back toward Tucson and forward toward his unknown future.

Thank You!

Hey this is Alex. If you have made it this far, Thank you!

I had a lot of fun writing this novel and I wanted to thank you for reading it.

If you enjoyed Iron Legacy – An Outlaw Biker Tale please consider leaving a review on Amazon as that would greatly help me out.

Please also check out my novel: Broken Brotherhood – An Outlaw Biker Tale

https://www.amazon.com/Broken-Brotherhood-Outlaw-Biker-Tale-ebook/dp/B0F2LMNBHD

I've a ton of stories in the pipeline if you want to keep updated on new books head on over to my website : www.alexmcrae.net.

Also feel free to follow me on Amazon here:

https://www.amazon.com/stores/Alex-McRae/author/B0F344WTHB

All for now

Alex

Arizona 2025

Extra special thanks to the following people:

Mooch, The Motorcycle Prophet, James 2, Hugo Dias and Jeremy Rogers.

www.ingramcontent.com/pod-product-compliance
Lightning Source LLC
Chambersburg PA
CBHW071508170626
46811CB00007B/2769